Bene
Bombe

by
David Webb

To Beth
Best wishes
David Webb

Illustrated by Kirk Bexley

First published September 02 in Great Britain by

Educational Printing Services Ltd.
Albion Mill, Water Street, Great Harwood, Blackburn BB6 7QR
Telephone (01254) 882080   Fax (01254) 882010
e-mail:enquiries@eprint.co.uk   web site:www.eprint.co.uk

ISBN 1-900818-337

Contents

Chapter 1

October 1940 - Nervous Days

'Now pay attention, children. Believe me - your lives could depend upon it!'

Mr Major banged on the huge, wooden teacher's desk with the flat of his hand to ensure that all of the thirty-eight children in Class 7 at St. Gregory's School were focused on his every word.

'Your gas mask should be in your box directly in front of you on your desktop. Do not open your boxes until I instruct you to do so.'

A small, grubby hand towards the back of the class crept sheepishly into the air and wavered slightly. It was William Snell. His face was turning pinker by the second as he waited for the teacher to notice him. Mr Major spotted the hand and said in exasperation, 'We've only just started, William! What on earth's the matter? Surely you don't want the toilet again?'

'Please, Sir - I've left me gas mask at home.'

There was a moment's pause before the storm broke.

'You've done what, boy?' The teacher took a

step forward, removed his glasses and glared at the quivering boy. 'You've left your gas mask at home? How many times do I have to tell you? You must carry your gas masks at all times. What would you do if there were a gas attack, William Snell? Would you rush out into the playground and shout Please, Mr Hitler - can you just hold on a minute - I've got to slip home and get my gas mask!'

The other children giggled, until The Major glared at them.

'I don't think so!' continued the teacher. 'I really don't think so, William. Well, you'll just have to pretend this morning, won't you? When we all put our gas masks on you can just pretend and we'll all laugh at you, won't we children?'

William, looking totally embarrassed, slid a little further down his seat and pulled the collar of his knitted jumper up around his ears.

The Major, as the children called their new teacher, took his place back behind the wooden desk ready to continue the gas mask drill. Their regular teacher, Mr Harris, had left at the end of Summer to join the Air Force and The Major was quite a contrast. Firstly, he was much older and he was certainly more strict. He actually looked like an army major, with his straight back and fierce moustache and he walked with a slight limp. There was a rumour going around school that he had been wounded while fighting in the First World War.

The Major took a deep breath and said, 'Now then, I want a volunteer to come out to the front of the class and show us all how to put on a gas mask correctly.'

A number of hands shot up immediately but The Major had already made up his mind.

'Simon Parks - you can be my volunteer today. Come on out to the front, please.'

'Hard luck, Sparky,' muttered John Harrison, as Simon Parks shuffled out of his desk, grabbed the cardboard box containing his gas mask and made his way to the front of the class.

'You should be good at this,' said The Major, pulling at his long moustache. 'After all, your father works at the army base up on Thornley Moor, doesn't he Simon? I'm sure you've had plenty of practice at putting on a gas mask.'

Sparky smiled weakly and clutched his box in embarrassment. It was a strange figure that stood before the children. Like The Major, Sparky had only been at the school for six weeks, since the start of the

Autumn Term. He had moved to Thornley from the South when his father, a research scientist, had been posted to the army base. He was a small boy, pathetically thin with a shock of red hair and a face that was spattered with matching red freckles, some of which were magnified by a pair of ill-fitting brown-rimmed glasses with thick lenses. He looked uncomfortable as he stood beside the teacher's table and stared out at the sea of faces before him. He pushed his glasses further up his nose and waited for the next instruction.

'Right,' said The Major. 'I want you all to follow exactly what Simon does. Open your boxes, please, and take out your masks.'

The children obeyed, Sparky placing his box on the teacher's desk.

'Now then, Simon, what do you do first?' The Major folded his arms and waited for a response.

Sparky thought for a moment and then he said, 'I take my glasses off, Sir.' And he nodded his head up and down so that they nearly fell off.

'Yes, yes, all right,' said the teacher, impatiently. 'Remove your glasses. What do you do next?'

Sparky took his glasses off and slipped

them into his pocket. Another moment's thought and then he said, 'I blow my nose, Sir. That's what I do next.'

The teacher looked perplexed. The children giggled.

'Blow your nose?' repeated The Major, slowly. 'You're in the middle of a gas attack, lad! You haven't got time to blow your nose!'

'But I've got a cold,' explained Sparky. 'I wouldn't like to sneeze inside my gas mask. That would be awful!'

Some of the children couldn't contain themselves and George Stoppard laughed out loud.

'Sneeze inside his gas mask!' he repeated. 'What an 'orrible thought!'

'That will do, thank you!' The Major's voice was raised. He was clearly irritated. He was beginning to realise that he had made a mistake in choosing Sparky to lead his demonstration. 'You can blow your nose quickly,' he said, relenting, 'for the sake of hygiene.'

Sparky removed a grubby handkerchief from his trouser pocket and gave a long, loud blow, which George Stoppard immediately copied. Sparky carefully returned the damp handkerchief to its home and, turning to The Major, he announced, 'That's much better, Sir.

Now I can put my gas mask on.'

The rest of the drill went smoothly. William Snell made a fair attempt at miming and even George Stoppard managed to complete the operation without too much fuss. Mr Major was satisfied that the children would survive the pretend attack, the gas masks were returned to their cardboard boxes and the morning continued as usual with a fairly dull mathematics lesson.

It was lunchtime. John Harrison and his younger sister Alice had gone home for their dinner and Sparky had joined them. Sparky lived just two houses away from the Harrison's, in Weaver Street and he was staying with the family for a few days while his dad worked up on the moors at the army base. Sparky had never mentioned his mother and the Harrison's had not liked to ask. He could have stayed with his uncle, who worked as a signalman at the local railway station but he had decided that it would be much more fun to stay with his new friends.

Mrs Harrison had prepared a cheese sandwich for the children's lunch and she had picked them each an apple from the tree in the garden. The apples were just right. It was the third week in October and they were perfect for harvest. It had been there years, that tree and even though its roots were disturbed when Mr Harrison had dug out the ground for the Anderson shelter, the crop was better than ever. Mrs Harrison had to squeeze around the metal shelter to get to the tree but the apples were too good to miss.

The children didn't waste much time. They finished their lunch, downed their drinks and set off back to school. It was a dry day, crisp and clear with just the faintest breeze dislodging the golden leaves from the tired trees that lined their route to school. There were piles of crispy, colourful leaves on the pavement and Alice kicked them up into the air as she skipped along beside the two boys. John was deep in thought and he turned to his friend and said, 'Do you think we'll . . . '

'Have another air raid tonight?' completed Sparky, adjusting his glasses. 'I don't honestly know. It wasn't really an air raid the other night, was it? I mean, I know we had to go into the Anderson shelter but the bombers weren't really over Thornley, were they? The planes were targeting Manchester.'

'I heard dad telling mum that we were in for it,' said Alice, joining in. 'And my dad's an Air Raid Warden, so he should know! He said there was going to be a bombers' moon for the next few nights and we'd be in for it!' She stopped with a puzzled look on her face and, tugging at Sparky's sleeve, she said, 'What's a bombers' moon, Sparky?'

'A bombers' moon,' repeated Sparky. 'It's

8

nearly a full moon and the skies are clear at the moment. If the bombers come over they'll be able to see their targets clearly, even if everywhere's blacked out.'

'I don't think I like the bombers' moon,' said Alice, looking up to the sky. 'I'd rather there were clouds.'

'I expect your dad's right,' said Sparky, thoughtfully. 'Although I don't know why the Germans would want to hit Thornley.'

'Maybe it's because of . . . '

'The railway line?' interrupted Sparky. 'Yes, I suppose it could be. I know the ammunition train goes through Thornley Station every so often on its way to Liverpool. I expect that would interest the Germans - if they knew about it.'

'I wish you wouldn't do that,' complained John, irritably. 'Why don't you let people finish what they're saying? It's very annoying.'

'Sorry,' said Sparky, and he pushed his glasses up his nose before thrusting his hands deep into his pockets.

The school playground was as noisy and chaotic as usual. Several children were standing in a circle watching two boys do battle over a game of conkers. One of the boys leapt into the air and yelled in pain as his opponent's conker rapped his knuckles. The onlookers fell about laughing. There was a hopscotch marked out in one corner of the yard and some of the younger girls were singing rhymes as each took their turn. Others were skipping, the long rope smacking the pavement as it turned relentlessly.

George Stoppard and William Snell had organised a game of 'Army' and their group seemed to be the noisiest of all as the children imitated the sound of machine gun fire and bombs dropping.

As soon as Sparky and his friends entered the playground, Janice Hogg came running up to them. She was a plump girl with a fright of wiry brown hair. Janice had started at St. Gregory's on the same day as Sparky and she seemed to have a soft spot for him, much to Sparky's embarrassment. Her parents had sent her from their home in Manchester to live with her grandfather in Thornley, hoping that she would be well away from any air raids.

Janice nestled up to Sparky and announced, 'My grandad says you can come to our house for tea tonight. Would you like that, Simon?'

Sparky looked horrified. His face turned visibly red, so that it matched his hair. He looked like a giant tomato. He shuffled uncomfortably and fiddled with his glasses. John and Alice giggled and nudged each other.

'I - I - can't,' stuttered Sparky, taking a step back. 'I'm - er - staying at John and Alice's house while my dad's at work. Mrs Harrison will have a meal waiting for me.'

Janice looked disappointed. 'Oh, well - another time then, eh? It would be nice, wouldn't it, Simon? Especially as we both started school together.'

'Yes - yes - another time,' agreed Sparky, and he nodded his head vigorously so that his glasses slid down his nose.

At that moment, George Stoppard and his gang came charging across the playground towards them. They had spotted Janice and they were determined to torment her. Several of them, including William Snell, had their arms outstretched in imitation of fighter planes and they whined like engines as they closed in on their target. Janice leapt behind Sparky and Alice joined her, leaving the two boys to repel the attack. George Stoppard had his gas mask on and he jumped up and down in front of Sparky and John as the pretend

11

planes circled the group.

'I'm an alien invader!' screeched George, his voice distorted by the gas mask. 'I'm a Martian with a hideous rubber face and I've come to invade planet Earth!'

'You're an idiot, Bus Stop,' said John, calmly. The other children had nicknamed George 'Bus Stop' because he was tall and thin and he had one ear that stuck out just like a bus stop. 'You don't need to wear a gas mask to look like an alien!'

'I've come to kidnap my victim and carry her off to another dimension!' He pointed at Janice, who cowered behind Sparky.

'Leave her alone,' said Sparky, stepping forward. 'Why don't you pick on somebody your own size?'

The planes stopped circling. William Snell sniffed and wiped his nose on his sleeve. Bus Stop whipped off his gas mask and glared at Sparky. 'Maybe I'll pick on you,' he growled, and he pushed Sparky in the chest, so that he stumbled backwards.

'That is quite enough!' snapped a stern voice from behind them.

The children turned to see The Major standing no more than a few feet away, his arms folded, his expression serious.

'I've been watching you boys from the

staffroom window.' The Major pointed an accusing finger towards George and his gang. 'Far too rough, all of you! Charging around the playground like a heard of wild elephants! And why is that gas mask out of its box, boy?' He glared at Bus Stop, who stared back defiantly. 'It is time you realised that your gas mask is not a toy! Now put it away at once and go and stand by the wall - all of you!'

Bus Stop glared threateningly at Sparky as he folded his gas mask into its box before slinking away slowly to stand in disgrace against the playground wall.

'Thank you, Simon,' crooned Janice Hogg, as The Major made his way back to the staffroom. 'I just knew you'd step in to save me. Thank you ever so much!'

Sparky looked at his friends, gave a gulp and shoved his glasses further up his nose.

Chapter 2

The Bombers' Moon

Sparky's Uncle Harry worked as a signalman at Thornley Railway Station. Sparky loved trains. He loved the noise and the smell and the hiss of the steam as it billowed across the platform. He had been glad to move up to Thornley when he heard that he was going to live near Uncle Harry, for he knew that he would be able to spend more time train spotting.

'You'll be able to come into the signal box with me,' Uncle Harry had promised. 'You get the best view of all from there, right along the line to the bridge. And I'll teach you how to work the signals. I'll train you up to be a railwayman, eh?'

He had kept his promise. Sparky had spent hours in the signal box, watching the steam trains journey in and out of Thornley Station, observing how his uncle controlled the signal, so that the trains took turns to cross the road bridge with its single track, slowly, carefully, giving a piercing blast on the whistle to announce their arrival at Thornley Station. Mr Bloch, the Station Master, didn't really approve of Sparky's presence in the signal box and he had made his feelings known to Uncle Harry on more than one occasion. Harry Parks, however, had been signalman at Thornley Station for more than fifteen years and he wasn't going to be told what to do by some young upstart who had only been in the job five minutes.

So Sparky continued to visit his uncle and Mr Bloch continued to scowl at him every time he arrived at the station.

This particular October evening was no exception. Together with John Harrison, Sparky had set off for Thornley Railway Station straight after school. His father had arranged for him to collect a package from Uncle Harry and John had asked to go with him, hoping to get an invite into the signal box.

'Don't you be too long,' Mrs Harrison had warned the boys. 'It's getting dark earlier these days and I want you home before blackout.'

It was cold and clear and even though the sky was still blue, the pale outline of the moon could be seen rising above Thornley Station. The two boys walked past the main office and Mr Bloch was out immediately.

'And where might you two boys be going?' he asked, sternly. 'There's a war on, if you hadn't noticed. I can't just let anyone walk through my station, you know.'

'I'm sorry, Mr Bloch. I should have knocked and asked permission. I thought you were busy,' lied Sparky. 'Is it all right if we walk down to the signal box to collect a package from Uncle Harry? We'll only be a couple of minutes.'

Mr Bloch stared from Sparky to John and then back to Sparky again, his huge, round eyes betraying the annoyance and anger he was trying to restrain.

'It's not good enough! I shall be having words with your Uncle Harry. I've been told to look out for suspicious people approaching the Railway Station - and it's not good enough!' Mr Bloch jabbed a stubby finger towards the two boys and then he said: 'Go on - and be quick about it! Make sure you're away from that signal box before the four-fifteen from Liverpool comes through. I don't want my signalman distracted when there's a train due in.'

Sparky didn't feel like a suspicious person but he said nothing. He smiled politely at the scowling stationmaster and turned to make his way along the platform towards the signal box.

'He's a bit fierce,' whispered John, as he

felt Mr Bloch's cold eyes watching him every step of the way.

'Take no notice of him,' said Sparky, reassuringly. 'My Uncle Harry says his bark's worse than his bite.'

The boys walked the short distance along the platform and then descended four stone steps onto a narrow gravel path. The signal box was a couple of hundred yards along the track. The lower part of the box was built of brick but the main section was no more than a wooden hut with large glass windows, so that the signalman could see along the track to the platform on his right and to the railway bridge on his left.

As the boys approached, they could see Uncle Harry, his dark silhouette outlined in the pale, yellow glow provided by a single light bulb that hung limply from a bare wire inside the box. That, too, was extinguished when the air raid siren sounded, so that the blackout was complete.

The door to the signal box opened and Uncle Harry stood at the top of the wooden steps.

'Come on up, boys!' he shouted. 'Watch the top step - it's a bit loose!'

Sparky climbed the steps and John followed behind. He didn't share Sparky's

17

love of trains but he felt quite excited as he stepped into the cramped signal box.

'This is my friend John Harrison,' announced Sparky, and he pushed his glasses to a safer position on his nose.

'Pleased to meet you, John,' said Uncle Harry. 'I think I know your father. Works for the A.R.P., doesn't he?'

'That's right,' said John, proudly. 'He's been down to the station a few times.'

'I'm afraid he could be busy over the next few nights.' Uncle Harry looked to the darkening sky. 'There's a bombers' moon rising and rumour has it that Manchester's in for another pounding.'

'They won't try and hit Thornley, will they?' asked Sparky. 'Surely there are more important targets?'

'Well, there is the army research base up on the moors, you know. And they could try and knock out the railway line. It does carry ammunition through to Liverpool. They hit an ammunition train in Liverpool last week - and one in Coventry the week before. There's an ammunition train passing through the station in the next few days. If the enemy get to know about it, anything could happen.'

'But how would they get to know about it?' asked John. 'Surely the information's top secret?'

'You're right there, lad,' agreed Uncle Harry. 'They don't even tell me until an hour before the train's due. Yet they knew about the trains in Coventry and Liverpool - right down to the last details. Now that suggests someone's feeding them the information, doesn't it?'

'You mean - a spy?' whispered Sparky. He wasn't sure why he was whispering. It just seemed right under the circumstances.

'Spies, traitors - call them what you want,' said Uncle Harry. 'Someone is passing on vital information.'

'Now I can see why Mr Bloch was so suspicious of us,' said John, quietly.

'Anyway, I've got a package for you,' said Uncle Harry, reaching down to a shelf beneath the signal controls.

He withdrew a small, rectangular parcel, tightly wrapped in brown paper and sealed all the way round with parcel tape. Sparky reached out and took it from his uncle, surprised to find that it was quite heavy for its size. He peered at it and turned it over, as if looking for a clue to its contents.

'Your father will come home to collect it from you within the next couple of days,' explained Uncle Harry. 'You make sure you

19

look after it for him - it's important.'

'What is it?' asked Sparky, and he held the package up and shook it gently.

'Don't do that with it, lad,' said Uncle Harry, anxiously. 'You could damage it. And never you mind what it is - you just make sure you don't lose it!'

'O.K.,' said Sparky, clutching tight hold of the brown package - but deep down inside he felt uncomfortable and more than a little suspicious.

Later that night the bombers came. John and Sparky were sharing the back bedroom, while Alice slept in with her mum. Mr Harrison was out on duty. He had left earlier that evening, at about 8 o'clock, dressed in his A.R.P. uniform. John had overheard him speaking to his mum as she had seen him out of the front door.

'Bill Hobbins reckons we're for it tonight,' he had said. He had tried to keep his voice low but John was listening from behind the kitchen door. 'All the fire crews are on standby. You see that you get down to the shelter if the siren sounds.'

'We'll be fine,' said John's mum, but she couldn't disguise the tremor in her voice. 'You take care of yourself, Eric. You make sure you come back to us safe and sound.'

The sirens sounded just after midnight, a steady wailing at first, that grew and grew until they screamed into the night. Mrs Harrison burst into the boys' room. She was fully dressed and she already had her long, grey coat on. Alice was behind her on the landing.

'Come on!' she urged. 'We've got to get to the Anderson shelter! They're bombing Manchester! They might come this way!'

John sprung into action quickly but Sparky was dozy and he wasn't too sure what was happening.

'W-w-what's that noise?' he stammered, pulling his jumper on back to front over his pyjamas. 'W-what's going on?'

'It's an air raid,' explained John's mum. 'You've no time to get properly dressed. Grab your trousers and let's go!'

'I can't find my glasses,' said Sparky, fumbling on the chest of drawers by the side of his bed. 'I can't see a thing without my glasses.'

'For goodness sake! You don't need to see anything! Just follow us, will you!'

The family hurried downstairs and out into the back garden, Sparky stumbling behind, his arms outstretched so that he didn't bump into anything. It was cold, freezing cold, and the night air made them catch their breath. A dog was barking and a baby was crying a few gardens further down the street, as neighbours made their way to their own shelters, the sirens still screaming their chilling warning. There was a boom in the distance, followed by another explosion and then another - but the bombs were still some way off, to the east, over Manchester.

'In you go,' said Mrs Harrison, and she pushed Alice in front of her, through the small door to the Anderson shelter. 'Watch the step down. I'll light the lamp once we're all inside.'

Sparky missed his step and stumbled forward, falling head first onto the damp floor of the shelter.

'Simon! Are you all right?' said Mrs Harrison, following him through the small doorway. 'Have you hurt yourself?'

'I'm fine,' said Sparky, picking himself up and rubbing his knees. 'Absolutely useless without my glasses!'

Mrs Harrison closed the shelter door behind her. She had a bicycle lamp in her hand, which she switched on once they were all safely inside. There was another huge boom in the distance, like a giant clap of angry thunder. Alice was sobbing quietly and Mrs Harrison pulled her close, reassuring, protecting.

Inside the shelter it felt cold and damp and it was very cramped. Mr Harrison had made two simple wooden benches, which ran along each side of the shelter. There were several blankets stacked on the end of one of the benches. Mrs Harrison had placed them there earlier that evening in anticipation of the raid. Mrs Harrison lit a small paraffin heater and passed a blanket to each of the children.

'Wrap them round yourselves,' she said. 'It could be a long night.'

Sparky coughed as the smell from the

paraffin heater attacked his throat.

'I don't like it,' whimpered Alice, her voice trembling with fear. 'What if the bombers come closer? And what about dad? He's out on duty. What if the bombers come closer?'

'I think we'll be all right,' said Mrs Harrison, putting a reassuring arm around Alice's shoulder. 'I don't think they'll come over Thornley.'

Sparky pulled his blanket tighter around him and glanced anxiously at John as several more explosions boomed in the distance. He was sure they were getting louder and, if he was right, it meant that the bombers were moving in their direction.

The explosions went on for another half hour and then there was a lull. They stopped, suddenly, and everywhere was quiet.

'Is it all over?' asked Alice. 'Can we go back inside?'

She had no sooner spoken than there was a new noise, a different noise, that sent a chill down Sparky's spine. It was a constant, steady drone and it grew and grew until it was directly overhead. Nobody spoke for a moment and then Alice said, 'What is it? What's the matter?'

'The bombers,' whispered Sparky, betraying the fear he felt deep inside. 'The bombers are overhead - and it's a bombers' moon. They'll be able to see because of the bombers' moon!'

'It's all right - they're passing over,' said Mrs Harrison, but as soon as she had spoken, there was a chilling whistling sound and seconds later a terrible explosion ripped into the night.

Alice screamed and clung on to her mother as a second bomb hit its target, the blast seeming to surround them, press in upon them. And then, as quickly as they had arrived, the bombers passed and voices could be heard, confused, shouting. Alice was sobbing again and both John and Sparky were shaking with fear.

'They've not hit the house, have they?' asked John. 'They've not blown our house up?'

'No, no - I'm sure they've not hit the house,' said Mrs Harrison, her voice trembling, 'but it was near. The explosion was very nearby.'

Suddenly, the door to the Anderson shelter opened and Mr Harrison peered inside. 'Are you all right?' he said, and his eyes darted from one to the other. Confused voices screamed out instructions in the background. 'They've hit the mill,' he continued. 'They were after the railway station but they've hit Thornley Mill! It's on fire, Emily! The firemen are there. I've got to go and help!'

'Take care!' shouted Mrs Harrison, as her husband backed away from the shelter and closed the door. 'For God's sake - take care!'

Chapter 3

Robbery in the Night

Three tired children trudged the short distance to St. Gregory's School the following morning. They had stayed in the Anderson shelter for another hour after the planes had passed over, frightened to go back into the house in case the bombers returned. Alice had eventually sobbed herself to sleep, exhausted as much from her crying as from the lateness of the hour. Mrs Harrison had carried her back into the house and put her to bed, still fully dressed with her wellingtons on. John and Sparky had remained awake for another hour. There was no way they could get to sleep. They had stood at their bedroom window and watched in disbelief as the flames from Thornley Mill leapt into the dark night sky, the billowing black smoke eventually blotting out the bombers' moon.

The burnt out mill was still smouldering the following morning. The children could see it as they made their way to school, the fire-fighters still damping down what remained of the building. It was a clear and frosty morning. The buildings, the trees, the roads and the pavements were covered with a black, sooty deposit from the charred mill, glistening like ebony snow in the morning frost.

As the children neared the school, a shrill voice cut through the cold air and made Sparky shiver more than the biting frost.

'Simon! Simon! Were you all right last night? After the air raid, I mean. You weren't too worried, were you?'

It was Janice Hogg. She had spotted her three friends and was heading purposefully towards them. She was particularly well wrapped up against the cold. She wore a long, black coat that buttoned up to the neck, a grey woollen scarf, a pair of knitted grey gloves and a matching knitted hat that buttoned under the chin. Her shock of wiry brown hair was doing its best to escape from beneath the hat, one clump sticking out like a well used brillo pad.

Sparky swallowed hard, took a deep breath and said, 'I was fine thanks, Janice. I was staying with John and Alice. We were in the Anderson shelter for most of the night.'

Janice pushed in between John and Sparky, so that she could walk by Sparky's side. 'I was worried about you, Simon. I know your father works up on the moors at the army base and I thought you might have been at home all on your own.'

'I told you I was staying with John and Alice,' snapped Sparky. 'Don't you listen?'

'Yes, well I forgot,' said Janice, 'and I was worried about you. It's nice that I was worried about you, isn't it, Simon?'

'Wonderful,' grunted Sparky, and he put his hands in his pockets and quickened his pace.

John and Alice nudged each other and giggled.

'Anyway, isn't it awful about the robberies?' continued Alice. She had broken into a trot in an effort to keep up with Sparky. 'Don't you think it's awful, Simon? About the robberies, I mean?'

Sparky stopped dead in his tracks and Janice immediately walked into the back of him.

'What robberies?' said Sparky, turning to face Janice. 'What do you mean *awful about the robberies*?'

'Haven't you heard?' said Janice, pleased to have Sparky's attention. 'Last night, while the bombers were coming over, several houses were broken into and robbed. Actually, I don't suppose the thieves had to break in. People would have left their back doors open when they took shelter. The thieves probably just walked in and helped themselves.'

'Unbelievable!' said Sparky, adjusting his glasses. 'Can you believe anyone could do such a thing?'

'Two houses were done in our street,' continued Janice. 'Mrs Lampard lives four doors away and she's had all her jewellery stolen. I'm glad we didn't go into the Anderson shelter.'

'You didn't go into the Anderson shelter?' repeated John, anxiously. 'You don't mean you stayed in the house when the bombers came over?'

'Well - yes,' said Janice, quietly. She was feeling awkward. She knew John's father was an A.R.P. warden and she was beginning to feel sorry that she had said anything.

'You can't do that,' said John, urgently. 'You could get killed. Look what happened to Thornley Mill. You wouldn't stand a chance if a bomb dropped on Cotton Street.'

Janice's eyes filled with tears. She looked at Sparky and then at John. 'It's Grandad,' she explained. 'He says that no Germans are ever going to make him leave his home. And it's Betsy, too. She's a bit slow walking and she's hard of hearing.'

'Who's Betsy?' asked Alice. 'Is that your grandma?'

'No,' said Janice, 'it's Grandad's dog. He pays more attention to that dog than he does to me!'

'I'll ask my dad to pay him a visit,' said John. 'I'm sure he'll see some sense and use the shelter next time. Now, come on, we'd better get to school. We're late already.'

The Major stood in front of the class, his arms folded, his face like a thunderstorm.

'I just do not believe it!' He paused for effect and glared at the tired children who sat in front of him. 'I just do not believe it!' he repeated, more slowly. 'Robbed in the night while the German planes flew overhead. I just cannot believe that anyone could be so callous.'

He walked towards the back of the class, between two rows of desks. The children kept their eyes fixed to the front.

'Oh, they took some money, the cowards who did this,' continued The Major, 'but more importantly, they took my medals from the First World War.' He moved forward again and stopped next to Sparky's desk. 'Can you believe that anyone could do such a thing, Simon? Can you believe it?'

'No, Sir,' said Sparky, quietly. 'I'm very sorry, Sir.'

The classroom door opened and Bus Stop tumbled inside looking dishevelled and dirty. He yawned and scratched his head and then closed the door behind him.

It was too much for The Major. His moustache twitched, his face turned red - and then he exploded.

'What do you mean by this, boy! How dare you crawl into my class looking like a rubbish heap! Have you no manners? Speak up, lad! What's your excuse?'

Bus Stop looked shocked. He pulled at his ear nervously, which made it stick out even more. 'I - I'm sorry, Mr Major. There was an air raid - and I didn't get any sleep - and then I overslept - and my dad's a postman, Mr Major - and he didn't wake me up - and, and . . .'

'Sit down in your place!' snapped The Major. 'Nobody wants to hear you rambling on, George Stoppard! And nobody else is late, are they, George Stoppard? The fact that your father is a postman has nothing to do with you being late has it, George Stoppard? He doesn't deliver you with the rest of the mail, does he? I take it he doesn't shove you through the school letter box?'

Sparky giggled - until The Major glared at him.

'Now, on this sad morning, we will carry on with our maths. Addition of pounds, shillings and pence, as I recall. Take out your books and carry on from wherever you left off yesterday.'

Later that evening, after they had eaten, John and Sparky went round to see Janice's grandad, together with Mr Harrison. John had explained about Mr Hogg's reluctance to use his Anderson shelter and Mr Harrison had been keen to visit him as soon as possible.

'We'd better get there straight away,' he had said. 'There's a good chance the bombers will be back tonight. They've hit Thornley once, they could easily hit us again.'

Alice had decided to stay at home. She was tired through lack of sleep and she was still upset from the events of the previous night. A walk through the cold, dark streets of Thornley did not appeal to her.

It was only a short distance to Cotton Street, past the school and down towards Thornley Lodge - a large stretch of water that had once been used to serve the cotton mills. The evening was cold and the huge, pale moon had already risen. There was a frost on the trees and on the pavement and it glistened in the clear moonlight. The streets were strangely quiet, as if people were waiting indoors in fearful anticipation of the hours ahead.

'It's a full moon,' said John, as they passed the school gates and crossed towards Cotton Street.

'Not quite,' replied Mr Harrison, looking to the starry sky. 'Two more nights before the full moon. We could do with some cloud cover but there's no sign of it at the moment.'

Cotton Street consisted of a row of forty-two terraced houses, each with a long, narrow garden at the back. Behind the garden fences was a patch of rough ground that led down to Thornley Lodge. The Anderson shelters had been put up at the bottom of the gardens, as far away from the houses as possible. Mr Hogg's neighbours had put his together for him, even though he had told them he had no intention of using it.

Mr Harrison knocked on the front door of number thirty-six Cotton Street and waited for a reply. After a few moments, the letterbox was raised and a pair of eyes peered out, curiously.

'Janice - it's us,' said Sparky, stooping down to the same level of the letterbox. 'We've come to see your grandad. We've got Mr

Harrison with us. We promised, remember?'

'Simon!' There was no mistaking the excitement in the voice. 'Hold on a minute - I'll open the door.'

A bolt was slid back, a key was turned and the door opened to reveal Janice Hogg beaming with pleasure.

'Come on in,' she said, pulling the door wider. 'Grandad's in the front room listening to the wireless. It's on a bit loud, I'm afraid. He doesn't hear too well.'

The group passed through the small hallway and into the living room. As they entered, Mr Hogg was sitting with his back to them, concentrating on a stern voice that sounded from the wireless. Sparky took the room in at a glance. It was warm and cosy and had probably looked exactly the same for the past twenty years, apart from the blackout curtains that were already in place across the small window. A coal fire glowed in the grate and a faded brass coalscuttle, together with matching tongs and a brass poker, stood on the hearth. Mr Hogg was sitting in a rocking chair, moving ever so slightly backwards and forwards, concentrating on the serious voice that came from the old wireless, which stood on top of a sideboard. There was a two-seater settee opposite Mr Hogg and a small, wooden table completed the furniture. An old, brown spaniel lay sprawled on the mat in front of the coal fire, one paw draped across its eyes.

KIRK BEXLEY ©2002

'Grandad - it's Mr Harrison come to see you,' said Janice, walking across to the wireless and switching it off. 'And these are my friends John and Simon from school.'

'Sorry,' began Mr Hogg, making an attempt to rise from his chair. 'I didn't hear the door go. I was listening to the latest news, you see. Pretty depressing, I can tell you. It's a good job my Janice has got good ears. Anyway, sit yourselves down. What can I do for you?'

Mr Harrison and John sat on the well-worn sofa opposite Mr Hogg. Sparky remained standing and Janice sidled over and stood next to him.

'It's the air raids, Mr Hogg,' began John's dad. 'I understand you're not keen to use your shelter? It makes sense, you know. What if Cotton Street had been hit last night? I probably wouldn't be here talking to you now.'

Mr Hogg took a deep breath before he replied. 'I know it makes sense,' he said. 'I realise that now. I don't mind admitting I was scared stiff last night - especially when I heard the mill go up. It's just that Betsy and I are getting old - too old to be wandering down the garden in the middle of the night.'

'And what about Janice?' said Mr Harrison. 'John tells me that her parents sent her here to get away from the worst of the bombing. You'd never forgive yourself if anything happened to her, would you?'

'No, I'd never forgive myself,' agreed Mr Hogg. 'I'll use the shelter from now on, I promise. And I'll make sure Janice and Betsy are in there with me.'

The old dog raised her head on hearing her name. She looked with bleary eyes at the visitors, thumped her tail twice on the mat and then went back to sleep.

'Thanks for coming,' said Janice, as Sparky followed John and his dad out into the cold, night air. She placed a hand on Sparky's arm and added, 'I'll never forget this, Simon.'

'No, I don't suppose you will,' said Sparky, and he pushed past John and Mr Harrison and walked away briskly up Cotton Street.

The bombers came again that night. The sirens sounded at the same time as before - just after midnight. Sparky was better prepared. He knew exactly where his glasses were. He had deliberately left them in his trouser pocket. There was no way he was going to stumble around in the dark again.

Alice was so exhausted that Mrs Harrison carried her down to the shelter. She sat on her mother's knee, wrapped in a blanket, and she hardly heard the bombs that boomed in the distance.

John and Sparky leaned against each other, wrapped in their own blankets. They talked quietly for a while but they, too, were tired.

'I hope Mr Hogg and Janice have got down to their shelter,' sighed John, and he yawned and nestled further into his blanket. 'And

Betsy, too. I hope they're in the shelter.'

'They will be,' mumbled Sparky. His eyes were closed, his glasses were slipping down his nose - and he didn't care.

Chapter 4

Suspicious Strangers

It was Saturday morning. John and Sparky were on their way to Cotton Street. They had agreed to call around for Janice and the three of them had arranged to take Betsy for a walk down by Thornley Lodge. The bombers had stayed over Manchester the previous night and, as there was no school, the boys had been able to have a bit of a lie in. They had left Alice in bed. John had stuck his head around the bedroom door to see if she wanted to join them but she had just grunted and pulled the blankets further over her head.

'Are you sure you want me to come?' said John, mischievously, as they walked past the school gates. 'Wouldn't you and Janice like to go for a nice little walk together? Just the two of you?'

Sparky didn't reply. Instead, he pushed his glasses further up his nose and gave John a stare that was colder than the morning frost.

The postman walked past them, his bag bulging with mail. John recognised him. It was Mr Stoppard - Bus Stop's dad. He scowled at the boys and almost knocked

Sparky into the road in his hurry to complete his round.

Janice was waiting for them. She waved frantically from the window as the boys approached.

'She's got her hat on,' said Sparky. 'I hate that hat. It looks like a tea cosy.'

The front door opened and Mr Hogg greeted the two boys. 'This is very good of you,' he said, 'agreeing to take Betsy for a walk. I'd take her myself but I'm not too good in the cold weather. I don't like Janice going down to the lodge on her own but with two fine young men like you to protect her, I'm sure she'll be fine.'

'Did you use your Anderson shelter last night?' enquired John. 'When the siren sounded, I mean?'

'Yes, I used the shelter,' confirmed Mr Hogg. 'Can't say I enjoyed the experience - and Betsy hadn't a clue what was going on - but we all used the shelter. You can tell your father I took his advice.'

The three children and Betsy the dog were on the footpath down to Thornley Lodge within minutes. It was unusually cold for the end of October. The sky was cloudless and clear blue but the thin sunlight had failed to shift the morning frost. It glistened on the grass and the bushes that bordered the lodge and the children's breath turned to mist in the cold, morning air. The ground, too, was frozen hard and there were patches of ice every so often near to the water's edge.

Janice had let Betsy off her lead. She was too old to run off. In fact, she looked as if she would rather have been curled up by the coal fire. She plodded behind the children, stopping every so often to shake her ears or to have a quick scratch.

'She could do with a hat like yours,' said Sparky, nodding at Janice's tea cosy. 'It would certainly keep her ears warm!'

Janice smiled politely, not too sure whether he was being serious.

'Look - there's a train coming,' said John, pointing towards the far end of the lodge.

Sure enough, puffs of white steam could be seen rising regularly in the distance, outlined like fluffy white clouds against the clear blue sky. At the same time, the two children could hear the steady rhythm of the approaching train. The engine and carriages came into sight and they stopped to watch as it advanced towards Thornley Station, slowing to a crawl as it crossed the old, stone railway bridge.

John gave a low whistle and said, 'That

looks really . . . '

'Amazing!' completed Sparky. 'Yes, it does, doesn't it. It's probably the ten-fifteen from Leeds. Thank goodness the bombers didn't manage to hit the railway station.'

Sparky took a few steps forward and then he stopped, abruptly. He stood absolutely still for a few seconds, frozen like a statue.

'What's the matter, Simon?' said Janice, moving forward to join him. 'Are you all right?'

'It's glinting,' said Sparky, and he adjusted his glasses so that he could see more clearly.

'What's glinting?' said John, joining them. 'Why do you always have to talk in riddles? Do you mean the train? I can't see the train glinting.'

'No, not the train,' said Sparky, impatiently. 'Over there, down by the footbridge. It's glinting in the morning sun.'

Sparky raised an arm and pointed towards the far end of the lodge. There was a flash of light, almost as if the rays of the sun had caught on a mirror and reflected back across the lodge, towards the children.

'I see what you mean,' said John, puzzled. 'What is it, Sparky? What's causing it?'

'I'm fairly certain I know what it is,' replied Sparky, 'but let's get a bit closer should we - just to make sure.' And he set off along the footpath as if he were taking part in a race.

John and Janice followed, leaving Betsy trailing behind, panting in the cold, morning air. They followed the narrow track along the edge of the lodge, heading towards Thornley Station, moving ever closer to the footbridge from where the mysterious light still glinted. And then Sparky stopped again, suddenly, and he raised a warning hand.

'I thought so,' he said. His voice was almost a whisper. He moved to the side of the track behind some low bushes, signalling for his friends to join him. 'Binoculars! There are two men on the footbridge and one of them is using a pair of binoculars. It was the reflection from his binoculars that was glinting in the sun. They're watching the train arrive at the station.'

'Well, what's wrong with that?' said John. 'Perhaps they're train spotters like you, Sparky.'

'John's right,' agreed Janice, peering round the bushes. 'There's nothing wrong with having binoculars, you know. My grandad's got a pair. He can see the railway track from his bedroom window and he often watches the trains.'

'It doesn't feel right,' said Sparky. He took his glasses off and rubbed the lenses with a grubby looking handkerchief. 'There's something suspicious about them. If they were train spotters they'd get much closer. They'd probably position themselves on the station platform so that they could get the engine number.'

'You're making a fuss about nothing,' said John, and he moved away from the cover of the bushes back onto the footpath. 'Let's go and take a look, should we? We might even find we know them.'

Reluctantly, Sparky followed his friend, while Janice waited behind for Betsy to catch up. The two boys were still some distance away when the figures on the bridge spotted them. One of the figures raised an arm and pointed, at the same time pulling at his friend's coat sleeve. They immediately turned their backs on the boys and scurried off across the footbridge, taking the path that led in the opposite direction around Thornley Lodge.

John stared after them, a look of total surprise on his face. 'I don't understand,' he said. He watched as the figures veered off the main path and took a side track towards an old, dilapidated building. 'They're going up towards Badger Farm. That's been deserted for years. The place is falling apart.'

'I told you,' said Sparky, smugly. 'Suspicious. Very suspicious. Mark my words, they were up to no good!'

The boys continued towards the footbridge as the two strangers disappeared behind a stone wall. One of them briefly popped his head above the wall, as if to make sure that they were not being followed.

The footbridge itself crossed a small stream that supplied water to the lodge. It was no more than a trickle at the moment as it had been dry for days. The bridge was raised slightly from the path and when John and Sparky stood in the middle, where they had noted the two strangers standing, they had a perfect view of the signal box, the railway bridge and the stretch of track that led in to Thornley Station.

'If they weren't train spotters,' began John, slowly, as he leaned on the stone wall of the bridge, 'then why were they . . . '

'Watching the train come in to Thornley Station?' completed Sparky. 'I don't know, John. That's the bit I'm not sure about.'

'Come on, you two!' shouted Janice from further down the footpath. 'Poor old Betsy's worn out and she's got to walk all the way home yet!'

'Sorry,' replied Sparky. 'We're on our way!' He was just about to move off the bridge when he noticed something on the floor, near to the stone wall. It was a rectangular piece of paper and it was smattered with a brown footprint where John had stood on it. Sparky bent down, picked it up and placed it on top of the wall. The two boys stared at it with interest.

'What is it?' said John.

'It's a timetable,' replied Sparky. 'It's a railway timetable. One of those two men must have dropped it in his hurry to get away.'

'I don't understand,' said John, scratching his head. 'What does it mean, Sparky?'

'I'm not sure,' said Sparky, picking it up and folding it in half, 'but I'm even more convinced that those two were up to no good.' And he slipped the timetable into his pocket and set off towards Janice and Betsy.

It was a slow journey back to Cotton Street. It had been a long time since old Betsy had walked so far and it was clearly too much for her. In the end, John picked her up and carried her, relieved to put her down again when they reached the gates of St. Gregory's School.

'I need to go into the corner shop for grandad,' said Janice. 'He asked me to get him some butter and tea.'

'We'll wait out here for you with Betsy,'

said John, as they approached the shop. He had quite taken to the old dog and he bent down to scratch her head.

Janice was just about to enter the shop when the door burst open and Bus Stop barged out onto the pavement. William Snell followed him through the door and William's older brother Keith completed the group.

'Well look who it is,' sneered Bus Stop, and he glared at Janice until she took a step backwards.

'Yeah, look who it is,' repeated William Snell. His nose was running even more than usual in the cold weather.

'Who is it?' asked Keith. He was a lump of a boy who always had a blank look on his face.

'It's Janice Hogg,' explained Bus Stop, and he prodded Janice on the arm with his forefinger. 'Janice Hogg who got me in trouble with The Major the other day.'

Betsy began to growl and John put a restraining hand on her collar.

'Leave her alone,' interrupted Sparky, stepping forward. 'It was your own fault you got into trouble. You shouldn't have been charging around the playground wearing your gas mask.'

'Who asked you, Carrot?' said Bus Stop,

49

turning to face Sparky. He did look a bit like a carrot. His face had turned red with anger.

'Yeah, who asked you?' repeated William Snell. He sniffed and wiped his nose on his coat sleeve.

'I like your hat!' continued Bus Stop, turning his attention back to Janice. He jabbed her again before reaching forward and tugging at the front of her woollen hat so that it slid down over her eyes.

This was too much for Betsy. The old dog lurched forward and bit Bus Stop on the ankle, causing the surprised boy to cry out in pain. William and Keith Snell backed away immediately, as John reached forward and took hold of Betsy's collar.

'It bit me!' moaned Bus Stop, and he hopped on one leg, clutching hold of his injured ankle. 'That old flea bag bit me!'

'I hope she doesn't catch anything,' said Sparky, seriously, staring down at Betsy. The old dog was still growling.

'You'll pay for this!' threatened Bus Stop, and he hopped off after his friends, who were already walking away down Cotton Street.

'Take no notice of him,' said Sparky, seeing the worried look on Janice's face. 'He's all mouth and ears! He hasn't got the brain to get his own back!'

Janice smiled and said, 'You're right, Simon. I'll go and get grandad's groceries.' And she opened the door to the shop and disappeared inside.

A few minutes later the three children and Betsy the dog were walking along Cotton Street back towards Number 36. Janice was just about to thank the boys when the door opened and, to her surprise, a tall policeman stepped out onto the pavement.

'Grandad!' she shouted, running towards the open doorway. 'What's happened? Are you all right?'

Mr Hogg was standing in the narrow hall. He was as white as a sheet and he had an anxious look on his face.

'I'm fine,' he said, as the policeman moved to one side. 'I've had a bit of a shock, that's all. I only discovered it when you'd gone, Janice.'

'Discovered what?' said Janice. 'What are you talking about?'

'We've been robbed!' said Grandad. 'In the night, during the air raid, when we were down at the bottom of the garden in that silly tin shelter!'

'Oh, Grandad!' cried Janice, and she rushed forward and threw her arms around his waist.

'He's not the only one,' explained the

51

policeman. 'Another half dozen houses were done last night, all of them after the sirens had sounded. We'll get whoever it is, don't you worry!'

John and Sparky did not know what to say. If they hadn't visited Mr Hogg with John's dad and persuaded him to use his Anderson shelter, the burglar would have probably left him alone.

'I'm really sorry, Mr Hogg,' began John. 'It's just that we didn't want you or Janice to get hurt, or Betsy, for that matter.'

'Don't worry, lad. It's not your fault. Anyway, they didn't get away with very much - I keep my few valuables hidden. They took my watch and chain, though. That belonged to my father. He gave it to me just before he died. It's not the cost, you understand - it's the sentimental value.'

'We'll do our very best to get it back for you, Mr Hogg,' said the policeman. 'Now if you'll excuse me, I've got two other houses to visit.'

By the time they arrived home, John and Sparky were feeling thoroughly miserable - but that was about to change. Alice was looking out for them from the front window and as soon as she saw them, she rushed to the door and flung it open.

'Guess who's here, Sparky?' she gasped. 'You'll never be able to guess!'

Sparky didn't have to try very hard. As soon as he stepped into the house he spotted his father's hat and coat on the stand in the hall.

'Dad!' he yelled, and he raced past Alice, almost knocking her over in his haste to reach his father, who was waiting for him, arms outstretched, at the end of the hallway.

Chapter 5

Back to the Lodge

'I wasn't expecting to see you until next week,' said Sparky.

They had all moved in to John's living room. There was a blazing coal fire and the room felt snug and warm after the morning cold. Mrs Harrison brought in a tray of tea and some homemade biscuits, which she set down on a small table in front of Sparky's dad.

'Help yourselves,' she said. 'I can't offer you sugar. We've finished our ration for this week.'

'That's most welcome,' said Sparky's dad, adjusting his glasses. 'It's freezing out there - and it's even colder up on the moors, I can tell you.'

He was exactly like Sparky. It was uncanny. He had a shock of ginger hair that looked as if it hadn't seen a comb for weeks; his face was spattered with freckles and he wore an identical pair of brown-rimmed glasses, which didn't seem to fit him very well.

'It's really good to see you,' continued Sparky. 'I remembered to . . . '

'Collect the package from Uncle Harry?' finished Sparky's dad. 'Well done, Simon. That's one of the reasons I'm paying you a visit. I need to take it back to the army base.'

Alice giggled. She nudged John with her elbow and he dug her back hard to stop her giggling.

Sparky's dad took a cup of tea from the tray and supped it loudly. It immediately made his glasses steam up and Alice giggled again.

'Now tell me,' began Sparky's dad, warming his hands on the hot cup, 'how have you . . . '

'Managed during the air raids?' completed Sparky, nodding his head up and down. 'Pretty well really. It was a bit frightening the other night when the bombers came over Thornley. They hit the mill, you know. It's been completely destroyed.'

'I know,' said Sparky's dad, and he took another loud sip from his steaming cup. 'We're not sure whether they were after the army base or the railway bridge. They weren't interested in Thornley Mill, that's for sure.'

'Why would they want to bomb the railway bridge?' asked Alice.

'To stop the ammunition trains from

getting through to Liverpool,' explained Mr Parks. 'They're getting information about the trains from somewhere. We can't understand it.'

Sparky immediately thought about the two strangers they had seen down by Thornley Lodge, watching the train arrive at the station. He pictured them in his mind as they hurried away towards the deserted farmhouse. He put his hand in his pocket and took hold of the folded timetable - but he didn't say a word to his father.

'There's an ammunition train due through Thornley in a couple of days,' continued Sparky's dad. 'We usually try to move them under cover of darkness but it's a bombers' moon at the moment. We might have to re-think.'

'Will the bombers come back?' asked Alice. 'Will they try and hit the railway bridge to stop the ammunition train?'

'We just don't know,' replied Sparky's dad. He took his glasses off and rubbed the lenses with his handkerchief. Sparky automatically did the same. 'One thing is for sure,' continued Mr Parks, 'we'll be looking out for them. And that's another reason I'm here in Thornley.'

'What - to look out for German bombers?'

said John, puzzled.

'Well, not exactly,' said Sparky's dad. 'But a German plane came down on the moors last night. It must have been hit during the air raid over Manchester and it managed to make it as far as the moors. We saw it coming down from the army base and we were out to it within fifteen minutes. The gunner was still strapped in his seat. He was in quite a mess. He had a broken leg amongst other things and he couldn't move. But the pilot was missing. He must have made off across the moors and, despite the clear moon, there was no sign of him. The soldiers are on the moors now, hunting for him. He could be in a ditch - but it's so cold that he's more likely to have looked for shelter.'

'You mean he could have come towards the town?' said John, slowly.

'Yes, it's possible,' agreed Mr Parks, and he nodded his head up and down. 'But I shouldn't worry. I can't see him calling in at Weaver Street, can you?'

'I don't suppose so,' said John, looking relieved, and he glanced across at Sparky, who was sitting absolutely still with a puzzled look on his face.

'Anyway, I'm off to Thornley Police Station,' said Mr Parks, replacing his cup on the tray. 'I need to make them aware of the situation.'

Half an hour later, Sparky was sitting on his bed, upstairs in John's room. He had said his goodbyes to his father and watched as his dad had placed the package carefully into his shoulder bag. John was on his own bed reading a comic. Sparky had taken the railway timetable from his pocket and he was studying it with interest.

'That's strange,' said Sparky, scratching his head. 'That's very strange indeed.'

'What's strange?' said John, glaring up from his comic.

'There's a date circled on this timetable. Monday 29th October.' He lowered the timetable and took his glasses off for a moment, as if to think. 'That's the day after tomorrow - and it's the full moon.'

'So what?' said John. 'Maybe somebody needs to catch a train on the 29th of October. It doesn't mean anything, Sparky.'

'My dad said the ammunition train was due through Thornley in a couple of days time. That would be Monday - the 29th of October!'

'You don't seriously think a muddy old

timetable dropped by a couple of train spotters has got anything to do with the Germans bombing the ammunition train, do you? It's ridiculous!'

'And they went off towards the deserted farmhouse,' said Sparky, taking no notice of his friend. 'We need to go and take a look around that farmhouse, John. We might find other clues.'

John stared long and hard at his friend. He put his comic down and shuffled to the end of his bed. 'You listen to me, Sparky. There is no way I'm going anywhere near that farmhouse. Do you understand? And if you've got any sense you'll stay clear as well. If you're really that suspicious about those two strangers why don't you tell your father about them? Or contact the police?'

'Oh, I will,' said Sparky, nodding his head up and down. 'Just as soon as I've had a look around that farmhouse.'

'Well, you're on your own,' said John, finally. 'You are definitely on your own!'

It was just over an hour and a half later that John and Sparky set off for the farmhouse. Mrs Harrison had made some sandwiches for lunch. She was planning a shopping trip to the town centre that afternoon and she asked the children if they wanted to go with her. Alice was keen on the trip and John was about to agree when Sparky got in first.

'No thanks, Mrs Harrison. We'll stay at home if it's all right with you. We've already been out in the cold today.'

John glared at his friend. He knew exactly what Sparky had in mind. 'You needn't think I'm coming with you down to the lodge,' he reaffirmed, as soon as his mother had left the room. 'I've told you - you're on your own.'

As the two boys threaded their way along the narrow path, John reflected on how weak willed he had become since he had met Sparky. 'I'm only here because I don't want you to be alone,' he said, trying to justify his presence. 'I still think it's ridiculous!'

'You could be right,' said Sparky. He gave a thin smile. He had known all along that John would come with him. 'Still, we'll check it out anyway, should we?'

It was a pleasant afternoon. Where it had got through to the ground, the Autumn sun had melted the morning frost but the more sheltered areas were still dusted with white. Most of the leaves had fallen but those that remained looked like golden decorations, delicately placed on the tall trees. There was a slight haze in the distance, beyond the railway line, out towards Thornley Moors. It was a sign that another cold night was on the way.

'I wonder if he's out there?' said Sparky, as he stared into the distance.

'What do you mean?' said John. 'Who are you talking about?'

'The German pilot,' said Sparky. 'I wonder if he's still out there on the moors?'

'He must be freezing cold if he is,' replied John. 'Especially if he spent the night on the moors.'

'I think he's still out there,' said Sparky. 'I hope he's not too badly hurt.'

The boys rounded a bend on the footpath and the bridge came into sight. Sparky stopped at once and raised a warning hand.

'What is it?' said John. 'What's the matter?'

'There - on the bridge,' said Sparky, and he stepped to the side of the path so that he was amongst the bushes.

John joined him. 'It's not the two strangers, is it?' he said, straining to see around the bushes.

'Oh, they're not strangers this time,' said Sparky. 'I think you'll recognise them all right. Take a look!'

John edged forward so that he had a better view of the bridge. There was no mistaking the three figures that stood out on the raised bridge, silhouetted against the clear background. John recognised Bus Stop first of all. He was tottering on top of the stone wall, his arms outstretched to help him keep his balance. It was obvious that the other two figures were William and Keith Snell. They were leaping around on the bridge, laughing and shouting and egging Bus Stop on as he walked the length of the wall.

'Idiots!' said John. 'What are they doing here? Shall we carry on past them, or what?'

'Let's hang on a few minutes,' suggested Sparky. 'They'll only cause trouble if we walk up to the bridge.'

The two boys watched from the bushes as Bus Stop and his friends continued to lark about on the bridge. They threw stones into the stream and Bus Stop beat his chest and made a peculiar jungle noise like Tarzan. The performance went on for longer than Sparky was expecting and he was just about to break cover from the bushes when Bus Stop suddenly disappeared over the side of the bridge.

'Has he fallen?' said John. He was more

curious than concerned.

'I don't think so,' replied Sparky. 'I think he jumped down to the stream. What on earth is he doing?'

'They've got something,' said John, moving forward slightly in an effort to get a better view. 'William and Keith have got hold of something. They're lifting it onto the wall and passing it down to Bus Stop. What is it, Sparky?'

'I can't make it out,' said Sparky, adjusting his glasses. 'They're too far away.'

'There - it's gone,' said John. 'They've pushed it over the wall.'

A moment later, Bus Stop's head appeared above the stone wall. He pulled himself up and scrambled onto the footpath. The three boys peered over the wall for a few seconds before leaving the bridge and heading off across the fields towards Thornley Station.

John and Sparky watched in silence until Bus Stop and his friends disappeared from view.

'Very strange,' said Sparky, 'but I think I'm beginning to understand. Let's go and take a look, should we?'

It took no more than a few minutes to reach the bridge. They stood in the same position as Bus Stop and his friends and peered over the wall. There was nothing unusual, nothing out of the ordinary, just a few marks and footprints in what remained of the white frost.

'Perhaps I was seeing things,' suggested John. 'Perhaps we should move on to the farmhouse and then get back home in the warm.'

'I don't think so,' said Sparky, and before John knew what was happening, he jumped up onto the wall and began to lower himself down on the other side.

'Take care,' warned John, 'the ground will be slippy.'

The warning came too late. Sparky lost his footing. His feet slid from under him, causing him to let go his grip on the stone wall. There was a stifled moan as Sparky tumbled backwards and landed on his bottom in the narrow stream that trickled under the bridge.

The moan was followed by a gasp of shock. 'It's freezing! I can't tell you how cold it is, John!'

'Well don't just sit there!' said John. 'Get out of it, you fool!'

Sparky scrambled to the side and sat shivering on the grass for a few moments while he regained his composure. John

couldn't help himself - he stood on the bridge and laughed.

'It's not funny,' growled Sparky, adjusting his glasses. 'Very damp and uncomfortable!'

'Well, was it worth it?' asked John. 'Can you see anything?'

'Oh, yes,' said Sparky, peering under the bridge. 'I can see something, all right. Very interesting. Very interesting indeed!'

John was beginning to lose patience. 'Sparky - what is it? What can you see?'

'I'll show you,' said Sparky, and he raised himself up and disappeared under the bridge.

John heard a grunt and a moan and the next moment Sparky reappeared, dragging a large sack behind him. John let out a gasp. He recognised it immediately. It was a postman's sack - the very sort they had seen Bus Stop's dad carrying earlier that morning.

'I don't understand,' began John, as Sparky stared up at him, and then a flicker of recognition came into his eyes. 'Surely not!' he said, taking a step backwards. 'You don't think Bus Stop and his dad are responsible for the robberies!'

Chapter 6

Trapped

'Think about it,' said Sparky. John had climbed over the bridge and joined him on the bank of the stream. 'Who would know the area better than a postman? Mr Stoppard would know every house and nobody would suspect him if they saw him carrying a sack around. After all, it's his job, isn't it? It's my guess he took Bus Stop with him to act as lookout. Remember how tired he was the other morning when he was late for school?'

'You're right,' said John, and he pulled at the rope that was bound around the end of the sack. 'Let's take a look inside.'

The rope came away easily and the two boys folded down the top of the sack. John gave a low whistle as the items near the top of the sack became visible. There was a clock in a dark, wooden case that had obviously stood on someone's mantle piece; there was a picture, still in its frame, wrapped loosely in a lace tablecloth; there were a pair of ornaments, delicate pink ballet dancers. Unfortunately, an arm had broken off one of the dancers, probably due to the rough treatment the sack had received when

William and Keith Snell had shoved it over the bridge. Sparky delved into the sack and pulled out a box. It was long and rectangular in shape. Sparky thought it was a jewellery box at first but when he opened it he let out a gasp, for it contained three medals, neatly pinned onto a cushion of black velvet.

'The Major's war medals,' said John, and he took the box from Sparky and peered down at the polished medals. 'They must be The Major's war medals!'

Sparky delved deeper into the sack and his hand closed around a chain. He knew what it was immediately. He pulled Mr Hogg's watch out of the sack and held it up in the air.

'Unbelievable!' said John. 'They must be hiding the sack under the bridge until they can get rid of the stuff. After all, nobody in their right mind would go scrambling under here in this weather. What are we going to do about it, Sparky?'

Sparky thought about it for a moment and then he said, 'I think we should put it back.' He watched as John's mouth dropped open in astonishment. 'I think we should tie it up and shove it back under the bridge.'

'But we need to tell the police,' argued John. 'They can arrest Mr Stoppard and return the stolen goods to their owners.'

'Exactly!' said Sparky. 'And we will tell the police, John - just as soon as we've checked out the farmhouse. We might come across some other information that the police need to know.'

It was no use John protesting. He watched in exasperation as Sparky wound the rope back around the top of the sack and pulled it into an untidy knot.

'There,' he said, admiring his work - and then he realised that he had not replaced Mr Hogg's watch and chain. He had placed it on the ground instead of putting it back in the sack. 'Oh, bother!' he exclaimed. 'Never mind - I'll put it in my pocket. I can show it to the police to convince them that we've solved the robberies. Anyway, we'll have to head back before it starts to get dark. It will be useful to keep an eye on the time.'

Sparky dragged the bulky sack back under the bridge and the two boys scrambled up the embankment onto the footpath.

'Right! Now for that farmhouse!' said Sparky, and he pulled at the seat of his pants, which were soaking wet and most uncomfortable.

It was a rambling old building that had stood unoccupied for years and was almost derelict. The farmhouse itself was no more than a ruin. The roof had collapsed; the windows were broken and the rotten frames were hanging loose or missing altogether; the front door had been kicked in and the entrance was overgrown with grass and weeds, browned by the Autumn frost. It was a sad remnant of a once fine property. Sparky and John stood in front of the ruin and stared at it in dismay.

'I don't understand what you hope to find here,' said John, quietly. 'We can't go inside, Sparky. It could be dangerous.'

'I think you're right,' admitted Sparky. 'I'm not really sure what I expected to find myself. It was just a feeling I had when I saw those two strangers heading this way.'

'Why don't we go home?' suggested John. He didn't like the place. He felt uncomfortable. 'You'd be able to change your trousers, Sparky. You'd like that, wouldn't you?'

'Yes, I'd like that,' agreed Sparky, and he pulled at the seat of his damp pants. 'Let's just walk around the back, should we, and then we'll head for home.'

'If we must,' sighed John, 'but I don't see what good it will do.'

The footpath that led round to the back of the farmhouse had crumbled and, at one point, the boys had to squeeze past a clump of overgrown brambles. At the back of the house was a large, open yard bordered by a stone wall.

John was getting irritated. 'Sparky, it's a ruin,' he said. 'There's nothing in there except bats and rats!'

'There's a barn,' said Sparky, completely ignoring his friend. He pointed across the yard to a separate stone building. He moved towards it and adjusted his glasses so that he could see more clearly. 'That looks in better condition, John. Let's take a look at it, should we?'

The barn was definitely in better condition. It had been sheltered from the worst of the weather by the great farmhouse on one side and by the stone wall on the other. As a result, it had survived the years relatively unscathed. Sparky approached the great wooden barn door and waited for John to join him.

'Do we have to?' said John, wearily. 'Do we really have to?'

A long, thick plank of wood lay on the ground to one side of the barn door. Sparky looked at it with interest and said, 'That would be used to lock the barn door, John. It fits across the front and rests on those metal brackets. Pretty solid, isn't it?'

'Very solid,' agreed John. He was totally
disinterested.

'And look up there,' said Sparky, pointing.
'There's a platform just below the roof. I bet
there's a hayloft inside. You can still see parts
of the winch that the farmer used to raise and
lower the bales of hay.'

'How interesting,' said John, and he gave a
wide yawn in the hope that Sparky would get
the message.

'Follow me inside,' said Sparky, and he

squeezed through the gap between the barn door and the stone wall. John followed reluctantly.

The barn was freezing cold. Strangely, it seemed colder inside than out. The two boys could see their breath as they stood inside the vast barn, waiting for their eyes to adjust to the dim light. There was only one small window in the side of the barn wall and that was filthy dirty and covered with cobwebs. Despite the cold, there was an unpleasant, musty smell of stale hay and general neglect. John's teeth began to chatter and he shivered violently.

Sparky moved further into the barn. There was not much to see. The rusty remains of some metal farm machinery lay propped against the barn wall and an ancient looking wooden hand cart with one wheel missing stood in the corner. There was a pile of old sacking on the floor, matted and damp and adding to the musty smell. There was a small wooden bench, broken at one end and there was a length of rusty chain curled like a snake beside it.

'Can we go now?' said John, his voice trembling with cold. 'I've really had enough, Sparky.'

But Sparky had spotted the loft ladder. It

was over in the far corner of the barn, a rough wooden ladder that led up to a storage platform beneath the barn roof.

'Yes, yes - in a minute,' muttered Sparky, and he walked over to the ladder and stared down towards the bottom rungs. 'That's strange,' he said, and he scratched his head and signalled for John to join him. 'That's really very strange, John.'

'It's a ladder,' sighed John. 'It leads up to what used to be the hayloft. What's strange about that?'

'There are fresh marks on the ground in the dirt at the bottom of the ladder,' said Sparky. He pointed to the floor and crouched down to take a closer look. 'Someone's been here recently, John. They've disturbed the dirt at the bottom of the ladder.'

John peered down at the scuff marks in the dirt and then slowly, very slowly, both boys raised their eyes to the top of the ladder and strained to see beyond, into the hayloft.

'What are you thinking, Sparky?' whispered John, although he already knew the answer. 'Do you think those strangers have been up in the hayloft for some reason? Or maybe there's another sack up there. Do you think Mr Stoppard's using it to store stolen goods?'

74

'There's only one way to find out,' said Sparky, and he put his foot on the bottom rung of the ladder.

'Take care!' gulped John. 'I'll follow you up.'

Sparky started up the ladder, slowly and steadily, testing each rung before he gave it his full weight. The platform was at quite a height and Sparky had never climbed a ladder before. He didn't like it. He could feel his heart beating and his mouth was dry but he made it to the platform without a mishap. He stepped off the ladder, relieved to feel the solid boards beneath his feet. Sparky held on to the top of the ladder and peered over the edge of the platform. John was already half way up. He seemed to scramble up the ladder with ease and he had joined Sparky within seconds.

The loft was quite wide but it was not as long as the boys had expected. It ran from the corner of the barn, where the boys had climbed the ladder, to a wide cross beam. It was dirty and dusty and the musty smell was even stronger. Several old bales of hay were stacked up against the far wall, white and powdery with age. One of the bales had split open and the dry hay lay heaped on the loft floor. A couple of old sacks were draped over the spilled hay. Sparky glanced across and was immediately suspicious.

'That's not right,' he said, pointing towards the sacks. 'Those sacks have been arranged on top of the hay. They wouldn't just fall like that.'

He took a step forward and then leapt back in startled horror as two, great black birds flapped from a roof beam right in front of his face. John let out a gasp as they veered past him and flew into the open barn before settling on the far side.

'Birds,' said Sparky, as if John hadn't noticed. 'They were only birds, John.'

John did not reply. His face was pale and his lips were quivering.

'Come and take a look,' said Sparky, regaining his composure. He signalled for John to move forward.

The two boys crouched down and stared at the frayed sacking. And then, suddenly, there was a new noise and it seemed to be coming from directly behind them. It was a grating scraping sound that echoed in the empty loft. The boys leapt round to see the top of the wooden ladder moving, sliding away from them. There was a crash as it tumbled to the floor and within seconds a choking cloud of dust exploded upwards, invading the loft.

'No!' screamed John, and he lurched

forward towards the edge of the platform. Sparky stumbled after him and the two boys stared down into the spreading cloud.

They could still hear something. There was someone down there, in the barn, shuffling around.

'Get us down!' yelled John. 'Don't leave us here! Please don't leave us up here!' His voice was hysterical, betraying the sheer panic he felt at being stranded in the freezing loft.

Sparky put a restraining hand on John's arm. He used his sleeve to wipe the dirt from his glasses and he strained his eyes in the direction of the movement below. The dust cloud dispersed and settled as quickly as it exploded and there, in the middle of the barn, standing motionless, staring up towards the hayloft, was a German fighter pilot.

The two boys stared down in horrified disbelief at the ghostly figure, which was covered with a film of grey-white dust. The pilot's eyes were wide with fright and, despite the dust, there was no mistaking the streaks of dried blood that clung to his face. They stared at each other for a few seconds - although it seemed like an eternity - and then the pilot took a few steps backwards, grimacing with pain as soon as he moved.

John found his voice. 'Don't leave us here!'

he cried. 'Please don't leave us!'

Slowly, the German pilot turned and limped towards the barn door. He gave one last glance upwards at the hayloft before he disappeared from view. The great, wooden barn door was pushed closed and the boys heard a groan as the wooden beam was dropped into position.

'I was right, then,' said Sparky, quietly. 'Someone was using the barn!'

Chapter 7

Escape

The boys were too shocked to move for a few moments. They stood at the edge of the platform and stared towards the bolted barn door. After the noise from the crashing ladder, the dust cloud and the frenzied shouting, there was an eerie silence. Eventually, John crouched down, glanced towards the fallen wooden ladder and said, 'Brilliant! What a mess! Thanks very much, Sparky!'

'It's not my fault,' protested Sparky. 'How was I to know the German pilot was sheltering here?'

'Not your fault?' repeated John, slowly, and he stood up and prodded Sparky in the chest. 'I didn't want to come here in the first place! Remember?'

'Yes - well - we need to get out of here, don't we?' Another film of dust had settled on his glasses and he wiped the lenses with his sleeve. 'Any ideas?'

'No I haven't!' snapped John. He was now more annoyed than frightened. He added sarcastically, 'You're the one who's supposed to have all the great ideas.'

'Just a bit stuck at the moment,' admitted

Sparky, 'but I'll work on it.' Sparky crouched on all fours and peered over the edge of the hayloft. 'One thing's for sure,' he said, 'it's too far down to jump. It makes me dizzy just looking at it. Anyway, we'd still be trapped inside the barn. We'd never be able to break the door down with that great post across.'

'We could scramble through the window, though,' said John. 'Most of the glass is missing, anyway. But it's no use while we're stuck up here on this platform.'

Sparky stood up and backed away from the edge of the platform. He put his hand in his pocket and pulled out Mr Hogg's watch and chain. 'It's three o'clock,' he announced. 'Another hour or so and it will be getting dark. It's going colder, too. I really don't fancy spending the night stuck up here.'

'Mum and Alice will be getting home from their shopping trip soon,' said John. 'Mum will panic when she realises we're missing.'

'There must be a way out,' said Sparky. He sat down on one of the bales of hay and scratched his head. 'There has to be something we can do.'

'What if we try shouting?' suggested John. 'If we both shout together someone might hear us.'

'Waste of breath,' replied Sparky. 'The

farmhouse is too far away from the footpath and the barn is round the back of the farmhouse, don't forget.'

'In that case, we're well and truly stuck,' said John. 'We may as well throw down a few bales of hay and make a bed for the night.'

'What did you say?' said Sparky, his eyes widening with interest. 'Say that again, John.'

His friend looked puzzled. 'I said we may as well make a bed for the night.'

'No, no,' said Sparky, impatiently. 'You said we may as well throw down a few bales of hay! Don't you see - that's the answer, John!'

John definitely did not see. He looked even more bewildered.

'Do you remember just before we came into the barn,' explained Sparky, 'I pointed out that platform near to the roof and I told you that it would have been used by the farmer to raise and lower bales of hay?'

'So what?' said John. 'How does that help us?'

'If there's a platform, there must be a door leading out to it,' said Sparky, 'from up here, in the hayloft. If we can find that door then we can escape, see?'

'No, I don't see,' said John. 'The platform was right up near the roof. We still couldn't jump down to the ground. We'd end up breaking our legs!'

'Not if we put the next part of my plan into action,' said Sparky. 'Let's find the door first and then I'll explain.'

The door was not easy to find. The one small window that had allowed the pale Autumn sunlight to filter through was down below them, at the opposite end of the barn. Outside, the sun was already setting and the temperature was dropping rapidly towards zero. The hayloft was dark and very soon it would be pitch black. The two boys started at one end of the loft, their eyes straining to see, their hands working along the stone wall, searching for any sign of a wooden door. After ten minutes, they had worked their way across the length of the loft - but there was no door.

'It's got to be here,' said Sparky. He was beginning to get frustrated. 'There was a platform outside. It's got to be here.'

'Maybe they bricked it up,' suggested John. 'When they left the farm.'

'Why would anyone bother to do that?' said Sparky. 'It doesn't make sense. No, it's got to be here. We've missed something obvious.'

'But we've felt along the whole wall,' said John. 'Except the bit behind the hay bales.'

'Of course!' said Sparky. 'That's it! I knew it was something obvious!'

John realised at once what he had said. 'The hay bales!' he repeated. 'The wooden door will be behind the hay bales! The farmer would stack the bales as close to the door as possible!'

Both boys leapt into action. There were about a dozen bales stacked against the wall. They were bone dry and dusty and the smell was awful. Sparky sneezed violently as they heaved the bales away from the wall, and his glasses flew off, slowing them down for a few seconds. One of the bales disintegrated completely as they rolled it over and the hay spilled out across the loft floor. But it was there! The door was there and the effort was worth it.

Once a space had been cleared, the boys rested for a few moments to get their breath back, sitting on the nearest bale of hay. They stared through the semi-darkness at the old, wooden door. It looked fairly solid but there was a large bolt near the top. Once that was slid back, the boys could get to the platform.

'Let's get on with it,' said Sparky, and he jumped up and tugged at the bolt. It wouldn't budge. It was so badly rusted that it wouldn't shift no matter how hard Sparky tried.

'Let me have a go,' said John, and he groaned and grunted as he strained at the stubborn bolt. The result was the same. The bolt would not shift. 'Terrific!' he said, giving up and wiping the rust from his hands on his trousers. 'We find the door and we can't get it open! Next idea, please, Sparky!'

'Haven't got one,' said Sparky, shaking his head. 'I must admit - I haven't got one.'

'Right, stand aside,' said John, and he took a few steps back and stared with determination at the wooden door.

'What are you going to do?' asked Sparky.

He didn't have to wait long for an answer. John let out a blood curdling yell and hurled himself at the wooden door, feet first. The door burst open and John flew through it, still yelling like a wild beast. He landed on his back with a thump and slid towards the end of the wooden platform. Sparky leapt forward and grabbed hold of the top of his jacket, pulling him to a stop just as John's feet dangled over the edge of the platform.

'You idiot!' said Sparky, dragging John backwards. 'You could have gone straight over the edge!'

'But I didn't, did I?' gasped John, and he pulled himself up into a sitting position. 'And at least we've got the door open.'

'Yes, at least we've got the door open,' admitted Sparky. 'Well done, John.'

'The question is,' said John, slowly, what do we do next? We're still stuck up here in the hayloft and it's just as far to jump down outside the barn as it is inside. We'd still end up breaking our legs, or worse.'

'I don't think so,' said Sparky. 'You see, I've already thought of that. We use the hay to make a soft landing. If we push the bales over the edge of the platform they'll break and spread out when they hit the ground. If we use enough of them there should be a nice soft landing for us when we jump.'

'Sparky, you're a genius!' said John. 'Let's get to work!'

The two boys got behind the nearest bale of hay and pushed it out onto the platform. The afternoon sun had disappeared, the light was fading fast and a pale, round moon was already rising in the sky. Sparky was shivering. It was not that he was too cold, although the temperature was already below freezing; he was really scared of heights and the moment he stepped out onto the narrow platform he felt dizzy. He didn't say anything to John. It was their only way of escape. They positioned the bale of hay on the very rim of the platform and then shoved it gently, so that it toppled over the edge. There was a thump as it hit the ground.

John peered over the end of the platform and grunted in satisfaction. 'Perfect,' he said. 'The bale's split open, Sparky, just as you said it would.'

But Sparky had already backed into the barn, away from the open platform.

They repeated the exercise over and over again until there were only two bales of hay left inside the barn.

'I don't think we need them,' said John, staring over the edge of the platform again. 'There's a great mound of hay down there, Sparky. It will be like landing on a feather bed.'

Sparky was shaking. He knew what he had to do next.

'Do you want to go first?' asked John. 'After all, it was your idea.'

'N-n-no,' said Sparky, quickly. 'You go first, John. I'll follow you down.'

'Well, if you're sure,' said John, and he sat down on the platform and dangled his feet over the edge. He shuffled forward, as Sparky watched in horror. 'Here goes, then!' He pushed hard and disappeared over the edge, out of view.

Sparky shut his eyes and took a gulp of

fresh air. An excited voice shouted from below.

'Yes! A perfect landing, Sparky! Now it's your turn!'

Sparky edged forward onto the wooden platform. He was shaking like a jelly and his legs felt weak and wobbly.

'I - I'm on my way,' he muttered, and he was aware that his voice was trembling.

Sparky sat down on the cold platform and shuffled forward, slowly, until his legs dangled over the edge.

'Come on!' shouted John from below. 'Get a move on, Sparky!'

Sparky felt ill. He dared not look down. He edged forward again, took a deep breath and then lurched forward into space. There was a rush of cold air and then a thump as Sparky hit the scattered hay. He coughed and spluttered and thrashed his arms and legs about, burying himself deeper in the dry, musty hay. Eventually, he stood up, still coughing, and wobbled forwards off the pile of hay. His glasses had been knocked to one side of his face and strands of dry hay stuck out from his hair and his clothes. He looked like a battered scarecrow.

'Well done, Sparky!' said John. 'A perfect landing!'

'Did you think so?' said Sparky, suddenly feeling proud. 'Nothing to it, was there?'

'Let's get out of here,' urged John, 'just in case that German pilot is still around.'

The journey back around the lodge to Thornley Police Station was difficult. Daylight had disappeared and, although the moon was rising, it was not an easy task to follow the footpath.

'What about the sack?' asked John, as the boys crossed the small footbridge.

'Leave it,' said Sparky. 'We'd struggle to carry it at the moment. Anyway, we can tell the police about it when we get to the station.'

Eventually, they came out onto the road, leaving the track at the bottom of Cotton Street. Sparky pulled out Mr Hogg's watch and chain. It was four-thirty. Mrs Harrison and Alice would be back home. They would have discovered that John and Sparky were missing and Mrs Harrison would be worried sick. Still, they had to get to the police station; they had vital information.

Five minutes later, the boys burst through the door of Thornley Police Station and approached the large, wooden counter. A rather plump policeman was pinning up a piece of paper to a notice board. He had his back to the boys and Sparky coughed to attract his attention. The policeman turned round and his mouth dropped open in astonishment. The boys looked like two dirty Victorian street urchins. They were filthy! Both boys were covered in dust and their faces were smudged and smeared where they had tried to wipe the dirt from their eyes. Wisps of dry hay stuck out from their clothes and their hair. In addition, there was a most peculiar smell about them.

'What on earth do you two want?' asked the policeman, moving to the counter. 'You look as if you've just crawled off the battle field!'

Before either of them could answer, the door to the police station flew open again and Mrs Harrison entered, looking pale and worried, dragging a tearful Alice behind her. She took one look at the bedraggled boys and raised both hands to her face in horror.

'John! Simon! What's happened to you? Whatever's happened?'

Chapter 8

The Bombers Return

John and Sparky gripped tight hold of their mugs of steaming tea. It was only now, as they sat in the safety of the interview room at Thornley Police Station, that they had begun to warm up. They were seated around a large, rectangular table, Sparky and John next to each other, opposite a kindly looking police sergeant. Mrs Harrison sat in the background with Alice on her knee.

'I think we'll make a start,' said the sergeant, but before he could ask the first question, the door opened and Sparky's father walked into the room.

'Dad!' exclaimed Sparky, his grubby face breaking into a broad grin. 'I'm surprised you're still here!'

'It's me who should be surprised,' replied Mr Parks, pulling up a chair next to the police sergeant. 'What on earth have you two been up to?'

John and Sparky exchanged glances.

'Shall I start?' said Sparky.

'Go ahead,' said John. 'After all, it was your idea.'

Sparky blurted out the whole story. He told

them about the two strangers he had seen on the bridge and how they had been quick to move away towards the deserted farmhouse when they realised they had been spotted; he told them about the railway timetable with the date, Monday 29th October clearly circled; he told them about Bus Stop and his friends and about the sack they had discovered beneath the bridge; he told them about the deserted farmhouse and about how they had entered the barn and climbed the ladder to the hayloft - and when he told them about the German pilot and their escape from the loft, Sparky's father looked startled and anxious.

'You could have got yourselves killed!' he stammered. 'I thought you had more sense, Simon. Why on earth didn't you tell me about your suspicions instead of putting yourselves into such a dangerous situation?'

Sparky looked embarrassed. 'Sorry dad,' he mumbled, fiddling nervously with his glasses. 'I was only trying to help.'

'You've given us a lot of useful information there,' said the police sergeant. He had been scribbling down notes the whole time Sparky was talking. 'I'm not sure where to begin!'

Sparky's father stood up and paced around the room. He looked anxious, his head bowed in thought. After a few moments, he turned to the boys and said, 'Do you still have . . . '

'The railway timetable?' completed Sparky. 'Yes, it's here in my pocket.'

Sparky withdrew the crumpled timetable and passed it over to his father. Mr Parks opened it up and studied it in detail. 'Hmm, that's worrying,' he said. 'The ammunition train is due through Thornley on Monday - and it's a full moon, a real bombers' moon. The date for this Monday has been clearly marked on the timetable. Why would they do that?'

'Perhaps the timetable has nothing to do with the ammunition train,' suggested the sergeant. 'Maybe the strangers were just innocent train spotters.'

Sparky's father didn't even bother to reply. He rubbed his chin and continued, 'You say the two figures you saw were watching a train come over the railway bridge and into the station?'

'That's right,' confirmed Sparky. 'They were using binoculars. We saw them glinting in the sunlight.'

'That's very worrying,' repeated Sparky's dad. 'That's very worrying indeed!'

'Can I get them home?' interrupted Mrs Harrison. 'The two of them could do with a jolly good bath. Besides, my husband will be home soon. He'll be worried if he finds an empty house.'

The police sergeant looked towards Sparky's dad, who nodded his agreement.

'That will be fine,' confirmed the sergeant. 'We'll need to speak to them again tomorrow. We'll probably ask them to lead us to the sack down by the lodge. I'll send someone round.'

'Off you go then!' said Sparky's dad. 'And no more heroics! Make sure you stay safe and sound!'

'Don't worry,' said Mrs Harrison, heading towards the door. 'I'll be watching them like a hawk from now on!'

It was six o'clock. The evening was freezing and a white frost was already beginning to form. As they were walking home, Mrs Harrison noticed that Sparky kept pulling at the seat of his pants.

'Are you all right, Simon?' she enquired. 'Is there a problem?'

'I - er - had a bit of an accident,' explained Sparky. 'My trousers are still a bit damp.'

'Oh, I see,' said Mrs Harrison, completely misunderstanding. 'Well, never mind. I suppose you were very frightened.'

'No, no,' said Sparky, quickly. 'Not *that*

kind of accident. I slipped and fell into the stream under the footbridge. I've had soggy trousers for hours. Very uncomfortable.' He looked at the sparkling frost and added, 'Not a good place to get frostbite, I can tell you!'

'Don't worry,' said John's mum, kindly, 'we'll soon be home in the warmth. You can have a hot bath and get changed.'

'That sounds really good,' said Sparky. 'I've gone a bit numb.'

Sparky put his hands in his jacket pocket to keep them warm. Mr Hogg's watch and chain was still there, in his pocket. 'I should have given it to the police sergeant,' he said, pulling out the watch and holding it up. 'He could have got it back to Mr Hogg.'

'Don't worry about it,' said Mrs Harrison. 'It will keep until the morning.'

As they rounded the corner of Cotton Street, Bus Stop and his two friends were coming out of the corner shop. Sparky shoved the watch back into his pocket quickly, so that Bus Stop wouldn't notice it.

'Don't say a thing,' whispered John. 'Don't give them any warning that we know about the robberies.'

'Hello Simon and John,' said Bus Stop, as he sauntered past. He had a sickly smile on his face, as if they were the best of friends.

'Hello Bus Stop,' barked Sparky, and he clutched hold of the watch in his pocket.

'Why do you call him Bus Stop?' asked John's mum, when they had walked on.

'Have you seen his ears?' said John.

'Oh, I see what you mean,' said Mrs Harrison, glancing round at George Stoppard. 'It's a shame, isn't it?'

As they neared home, the front door opened and Mr Harrison peered up the road towards them. 'Where on earth have you all been?' he said, anxiously, and then spotting the state of the two boys, he added, 'And what have you two been up to? You look as if you've just come off a battlefield!'

'It's a long story,' said his wife, quietly. 'Let's get inside and I'll tell you all about it!'

It was more of a discussion than an argument but voices were definitely raised. John was in the bath and the bathroom door was closed. Alice had already gone to bed, tired out by the cold and the events of the day. Sparky sat down quietly at the top of the stairs and tuned in as Mr Harrison made his feelings clear.

'I blame that boy!' he snapped. 'Our John would never have gone off on his own like that. He knows better. I'm telling you, that boy is leading him astray! There's something funny about him!'

'That's unfair,' retorted Mrs Harrison. 'He was doing what he thought was right. He was only trying to help. And after all, he has given the police some vital information.'

'And where's he come from?' continued Mr Harrison. He had begun to pace up and down in an agitated manner. 'We don't know anything about him - or his father, for that matter. All this nonsense about secret work at the army base. I feel very uneasy about it, I can tell you!'

'I'm sure both boys will have learnt their lesson,' said Mrs Harrison. 'Everyone makes mistakes, you know, Eric. Have you never made a mistake?'

'You can't afford to make mistakes at the moment,' retorted Mr Harrison. 'Mistakes cost lives; you know that, Jane.'

'I'm sure you're over-reacting,' said Mrs Harrison, doing her best to remain calm. 'Anyway, it won't happen again, Eric. We'll make sure of that.'

'We certainly will,' said Mr Harrison. 'One more episode like today's fiasco and that boy will be out of this house. He can go and stay with his uncle. We've got enough to do looking after our own children.'

'Yes, well you might see things differently when you've calmed down a bit,' said Mrs Harrison. 'Now you get off to work and stop worrying.'

'Oh - I'm sorry,' said Mr Harrison, his voice softening. 'It's just that it's such a worrying time at the moment. Perhaps I have been a little harsh on the lad. I don't want anyone to get hurt, you know that. I think too much of you all. We're expecting more air raids over the next few nights and I'm a little bit tense.'

'I know,' said his wife, and she kissed him on the forehead. 'We'll get down to the shelter if there's a problem. You take care of yourself.'

Sparky heard the front door open and then bang shut as Mr Harrison left for duty. He took a deep breath and then stood up slowly. Before he could move, Mrs Harrison started up the stairs. She stopped half way as she saw Sparky staring down at her, his face pale, his eyes wide.

'I'm sorry,' said Sparky, and his voice quivered with emotion. 'It was all my fault. I was stupid. I led us both into danger.'

John's mum didn't answer. Instead, she held out her arms. He took the few steps down to meet her and, as he rested his head on her shoulder, he could feel the tears welling in his eyes. He had never known his own mother. He could not remember the last time he had been hugged.

That night the bombers returned. It was nine o'clock when the sirens sounded - the earliest warning yet. Sparky and John had just finished their supper of toast and tea and had gone up to their room when Mrs Harrison burst through the door.

'We need to get down to the shelter,' she urged. 'Your father said there'd be raids. You two boys make a start while I see to Alice.'

Sparky and John didn't waste any time. They had not got changed for bed and so they were fully dressed. They made their way downstairs and waited for Mrs Harrison and Alice by the kitchen door. John's mum was with them within a minute, dragging a blurry-eyed Alice behind her.

'I'm fed up of the bombers,' moaned Alice. 'Why don't they go and bomb somewhere else?'

Mrs Harrison grabbed Alice's coat from the back of a kitchen chair and wrapped it around her shoulders. 'It won't go on forever,' she said, doing her best to reassure the little girl. 'We've just got to be brave and sensible at the moment.' Turning to John, she said, 'Will you bring the cardboard box from the kitchen table. I've made up a flask of tea and some sandwiches. I've got a feeling it's going to be a long night!'

The Anderson shelter was freezing cold. Mrs Harrison lit the small paraffin heater but it did not make a great deal of difference. They sat there, the four of them, with blankets wrapped around their shoulders, listening for the first hint of the bombers arriving.

It was strange. Sparky couldn't understand it at first. The last few times they had used the shelter they had heard the explosions in the distance as the planes dropped their bombs on Manchester but this time, there was nothing, just an eerie silence.

'Are you sure the bombers are coming?' asked Alice. 'It doesn't sound as if the bombers are coming.'

'Listen!' said Mrs Harrison, and they strained their ears to pick up the distant sound.

'I can hear it,' whispered Sparky, his voice trembling with fear.

It started as a distant drone that grew steadily louder as the planes approached. John and Sparky exchanged glances but they did not have to say anything.

'Why can't we hear the bangs?' asked Alice. 'Over Manchester?'

'I don't think Manchester is the target tonight,' replied Mrs Harrison. 'I think they want to hit Thornley.'

The first explosion took them by surprise. There was no whistling sound, just a tremendous blast as the bomb hit its target somewhere across Thornley. The boys jerked backwards on their bench and Mrs Harrison clung hold of Alice. The first blast was followed by a second and then another and yet another. Alice cried out in fright and buried her head into her mother's shoulder. In the distance, voices shouted and screamed and an air raid siren started up again, wailing into the night, far too late to be of any use, adding to the noise and the chaos. Another bomb dropped and the explosion ripped into the night. It was nearer - much nearer. The top of the Anderson shelter was spattered with debris as the occupants cowered beneath the thin, metal roof. Alice screamed as yet another bomb whistled through the air and vented its anger nearby. It was terrifying. Sparky had never known such terror. He couldn't speak. He couldn't cry out in fear. He just sat there, clutching hold of John, who was shaking with fright.

More bombs fell but it was clear that the planes were passing over, for the explosions became more distant and less frequent.

'We're all right,' said Mrs Harrison, her voice still trembling. 'They're passing over and we're all right.'

'They've hit the house!' wailed Alice. 'I know they've hit the house. I could hear things landing on top of the shelter.'

'No, not our house,' said Mrs Harrison. 'It would have been much worse if they'd hit our house. But they've hit somewhere nearby, that's for sure. Stay here while I take a look outside.'

Mrs Harrison pulled away from Alice's tight grip and turned the metal handle on the door of the Anderson shelter. She pushed against the door but it wouldn't give at first. 'Something's landed right outside,' she said. 'The door won't open.' She shoved against the door with her shoulder and it moved slowly, with a grating, scraping sound.

There were no more explosions. The planes had moved on, their mission complete. But there were voices; frightened, confused voices, shouting instructions and asking questions. And there was a red glow in the sky. The children could see it from inside the shelter, through the open doorway, and they knew at once that somewhere nearby was burning.

Mrs Harrison stepped out of the shelter and stared towards the red glow and, as she did so, her husband appeared from around the side of the house.

'Thank God you're all right,' he said, as he rushed towards her. 'We were waiting near the station but they were well off target.'

'Is it the school, Eric? The red glow in the sky? Have they hit the school?'

'No, it's not the school,' replied Mr Harrison. 'It was a near thing, though. I'm afraid they've hit Cotton Street. There are at least three houses gone.'

Chapter 9

Janice's Story

Janice and her grandfather knew nothing about the expected air raids. They, too, had been shopping in Thornley town centre earlier that Saturday afternoon, leaving Betsy curled up on the rug in front of the fire. Mr Hogg had bought Janice a new jumper, a thick woolly jumper with a high neck, bright red in colour.

'It'll keep you nice and warm in this weather,' he had said. 'Especially if we have to go out in the middle of the night and sit in that silly shelter. It's a pity they haven't got one to fit Betsy, too!'

He had taken his best shoes to be mended at the cobblers and they had gone to the tea rooms for a hot drink and a toasted tea cake.

Janice enjoyed spending time with her grandfather. Although she had seen him regularly before the war, she had seldom stayed with him. He usually came across Manchester to visit her at home, bringing Betsy on the train with him. Janice loved old Betsy. Her mum and dad wouldn't let her have a dog of her own and so a visit from grandfather and Betsy was something special. 'You can share her,' grandfather would say. 'We'll say she's yours as well as mine, should we?' And Janice was satisfied with that. She told everyone at her school that she had an old, brown spaniel called Betsy, and she got annoyed when some of her friends made fun of her.

They did not have much of an evening meal. Janice finished off the vegetable soup that her grandad had made the day before, and Mr Hogg warmed up the remaining half of a meat pie that he had bought from Gregson's butchers a few days earlier.

Janice had pulled a face at the pie when her grandad had offered it to her. 'It's not very fresh, you know,' she had warned. 'And mum says you should never reheat a pie; it can make you ill.'

'Your mother's a fusspot,' retorted grandad. 'Always was and always will be. I say you should never waste good food - and this pie's no exception. It tastes fine to me.'

In truth, Mr Hogg thought it tasted a bit peculiar but there was no way he was going to admit that to his granddaughter and so he persevered with his meal, slipping the occasional piece of pie underneath the table for Betsy.

Janice did the washing up, carefully

boiling a kettle of water on the gas stove and pouring it over the dishes in the old, stone sink. By the time she had dried the dishes and put them back on the kitchen shelves, her grandfather was asleep, snoring gently in his favourite chair opposite the coal fire, some background music crackling quietly from the wireless. Janice had to smile. Betsy, too, was asleep, curled up on the rug, as close as she could get to the warmth of the fire. Her tail was actually in the grate and Janice lifted it back onto the mat to stop it from singeing.

It was only six-thirty. It was going to be a long evening. Janice went up to her room and brought down a *Just William* book she was reading. She turned the sound down on the wireless so that it was barely audible and she settled down on the settee to read her book.

It was after about an hour that her grandad began to make some peculiar noises. The snoring had got steadily heavier and at one point it was as if he and Betsy were having a snoring competition. Janice was finding it difficult to concentrate on her book. But then her grandad began to grunt and groan and, as he became more restless, his head tossed from side to side. At first, Janice thought he was dreaming, especially as he appeared to mutter something at one point.

But the groaning seemed to become more troubled and Janice couldn't help but notice the sweat that had broken out on her grandad's forehead. At the same time, she noticed that Betsy was no longer snoring, she was panting, with her eyes open and her tongue hanging out.

Janice knew that there was something wrong - but she wasn't sure what to do about it. She got up from the settee and approached her grandad. She placed a hand on his arm and shook him gently.

'Grandad! Grandad! Are you all right?'

Mr Hogg took in a deep breath and then groaned again. Janice shook him a little harder.

'Grandad! Wake up grandad! What's the matter?'

The old man's eyes opened and he stared straight ahead, as if he was looking right through Janice. And then he seemed to realise where he was and his eyes focused on her face.

'Janice,' he mumbled, 'what are you doing here? I don't feel so good. Most peculiar!'

'You've been moaning in your sleep, grandad. And you're hot. I'm sure it's that pie you ate up. It's made you ill.'

Mr Hogg leaned forward in his chair and

placed one hand on his stomach. 'You could be right, Janice. Terrible stomach ache - and I feel a bit sick.'

'But I don't understand about Betsy,' said Janice, puzzled.

'What do you mean?' asked grandad, sounding suddenly alarmed.

'Look at her,' said Janice, pointing towards the panting dog. 'She looks all hot and bothered the same as you.'

'Oh, no,' said grandad, sinking back in his chair. 'What have I done?'

Janice realised the truth immediately. 'You fed Betsy some of that pie, didn't you grandad? You slipped it under the table when I wasn't looking.'

The old man now looked guilty as well as ill. 'Yes, I did,' he admitted, and he took in a big gulp of air. 'Only a few bits of meat, mind. You know I'd never do anything to harm old Betsy.'

'I know that,' said Janice, gently. 'And I'm sure she'll get over it. Why don't you go up to bed and I'll get a bowl of fresh water for Betsy? I'd better act as a nurse for both of you!'

'Yes, I think I will,' agreed grandad, and he stood up unsteadily and wobbled towards the door.

'And perhaps you'll listen to me next time,' added Janice. She was beginning to enjoy herself. It wasn't often she got the final word.

'You sound just like your mother,' said grandad, as he disappeared through the door. 'She was a bossy little madam when she was your age!'

Janice was still up when the sirens sounded. She had given Betsy a bowl of water, which the old dog had lapped up on the rug in front of the fire, and she had settled back down on the settee to read some more of her book. She had checked on her grandad at eight-thirty and found him lying, fully dressed, on top of his bed - but at least he appeared to be sleeping more peacefully. The sound of the siren wailing its warning into the night, building to a steady crescendo, sent a shiver down her spine and, suddenly, she was no longer feeling quite so confident, no longer feeling in control.

Betsy didn't move. Her ears twitched slightly but the chilling warning was lost somewhere on the way to her brain.

Janice stirred herself into action. She tossed her book aside and pulled her slippers back on. For some reason, she glanced at the clock on the mantelpiece on her way out of the room. 'Nine o'clock,' she said out loud. 'It's too early for the bombers to come. What are they playing at?'

Janice took the stairs two at a time and burst into her grandad's room. He was still fast asleep on the bed. He hadn't moved. This time, she didn't shake him gently, she pushed against his side and rocked him backwards and forwards.

'Grandad! Wake up! Quickly! The sirens are sounding!'

Mr Hogg groaned loudly and opened his eyes. He thought he was having a nightmare.

'The sirens?' he repeated. 'They can't be! What time is it?'

'Never mind the time,' urged Janice, tugging at him until he raised himself into a sitting position. 'The bombers are coming. We've got to get down to the shelter.' And then she added, 'It's nine o'clock!'

'Nine o'clock!' spluttered grandad. 'Nine o'clock! That's ridiculous! The bombers won't come at nine o'clock. It must be a mistake!'

Janice was pleading with him. 'It's not a mistake, grandad! We can't take the risk! Please let's go to the shelter!'

'Yes - yes,' said grandad, 'we'll go to the shelter. Let me find my shoes. I just feel a bit

111

groggy. I think it was that pie.'

'You've got your shoes on, grandad! Hurry up! Please hurry up!'

Janice helped her grandad downstairs and they collected their coats from the hall cupboard. The sirens had been sounding for five minutes and still they wailed, until Janice wasn't sure whether the sound was outside or somewhere deep inside her head. They kept the lights off. Grandad had a small torch in his coat pocket and the two of them used it to find their way through the small kitchen to the back door. Janice opened the door to be met immediately by a blast of ice cold air. The wail from the sirens was even louder and Janice could hear someone shouting a few gardens away.

'Wait,' said grandad, 'we've forgotten Betsy. We can't go without Betsy.'

'I'll go for her,' said Janice, and she grabbed the torch from her grandad and made her way back through the kitchen.

Betsy was still asleep on the rug. She had put one paw across her ears, as if to shut out the troublesome siren.

'Come on, old girl,' said Janice, and she shifted the dog's paw and scratched her head. 'Come on, Betsy, there's an air raid.'

The old dog opened her eyes and yawned

but made no effort to raise herself.

'Come on,' urged Janice, and she tugged at the dog's collar for encouragement.

Reluctantly, Betsy rolled over, staggered to her feet and shook herself. Janice took hold of her collar and pulled her towards the door. Betsy began to pant again. She clearly wasn't well.

'I've got her,' shouted Janice, arriving back in the kitchen. 'We'll follow you down to the shelter, grandad.'

Mr Hogg stepped outside and Janice followed, coaxing and encouraging Betsy with every step. She tried to pull the back door closed behind her but it was difficult with one hand on Betsy's collar.

'Leave it,' said grandad. 'I've nothing left to steal.'

Suddenly, the sirens stopped and for an instance, the night was still. It didn't last long. Before they were half way down the garden path a new, chilling sound cut into the silence. Janice stopped and listened and her grandad came to a halt on the narrow garden path beside her.

'What is it?' said grandad. 'Why have you stopped?'

'Listen!' said Janice, a distinct tremble in her voice. 'The bombers, grandad. They're nearby.' The low drone grew louder and louder until there was no mistaking the threat. 'Come on, grandad! We've got to get to the shelter!' But as she moved forward again she lost her grip on Betsy's collar and the dog, frightened by the noise, turned before she knew what was happening and headed back down the path towards the dark house. Janice and grandad watched helplessly as she disappeared through the open kitchen door.

KIRK BEXLEY ©?

'Leave her,' said grandad. 'She'll be all right. She'll find a place to hide.'

The very next moment there was a long, shrill whistle, which was followed by a tremendous explosion. A bomb had dropped across Thornley and Janice and her grandad stared in horror as the sky to the east was lit with an instant orange glow.

'The shelter,' snapped grandad, and he took hold of Janice's arm and dragged her the remaining distance along the path to the Anderson shelter door.

They were inside within seconds as another explosion, and then another ripped into the night. Mr Hogg had put two old, wooden chairs inside the shelter and they sat there, side by side, Janice snuggling in to her grandad's great coat as the bombs continued to drop and the explosions tore into the night.

'I can't understand it,' said grandad. There was a lull in the bombing. 'Why are they bombing a small town like Thornley? I can see why they want to hit Manchester but why Thornley?'

Janice had no time to reply. There was a sudden loud whistling sound and the resultant explosion threw them off their seats and onto the floor of the shelter. The explosion seemed to go on forever. The very ground shook and bricks and debris rained down on top of the shelter. Another bomb hit Cotton Street and it was as if an earthquake had struck. Janice screamed and screamed but her screams were lost in the noise and confusion that surrounded her. Through the confusion, she could hear her grandfather's voice calling her name, over and over again, but she couldn't reply. She just lay there on the ground, shaking with sheer panic. And then she was in her grandad's arms. He had picked her up and he was holding her close, kneeling on the damp floor of the shelter. The bombers had passed over and only their devastation remained.

They didn't move for a few minutes. Janice and her grandad, holding each other inside the shelter. They were encased in total darkness. And then there was more confusion outside. They could hear voices shouting and screaming and snapping out orders.

'The house has gone . . . '

'Must have been a direct hit . . . '

'Was there anyone inside?'

It was Janice who found her voice first. She pulled away from her grandad and hammered on the Anderson shelter door.

'We're in here! Help us, somebody! We're inside the shelter!'

More voices and then a frantic scramble as bricks and rubble were pulled away from the entrance to the shelter.

'We're in here!' yelled Janice, hysterically. 'Get us out! Please get us out!'

The door was dragged open and a bright torch beam cut into the darkness.

'They're all right,' said a voice. 'There's two of them and they're all right.'

John's dad stepped into the shelter and a second A.R.P. warden passed some blankets through the semi-open door.

'It's all right,' said Mr Harrison, wrapping one of the blankets around Janice, 'there's an ambulance on the way. You're going to be all right.'

'The house?' said Janice's grandad, his voice still shaking. 'What about my house?'

There was a pause before Mr Harrison answered.

'I'm afraid the house is gone.'

Janice's grandad put his head in his hands in an awful moment of realisation.

'Betsy . . . .' he said quietly. 'Betsy went back inside the house.'

Chapter 10

The Following Day

It was breakfast time before Mr Harrison arrived home that Sunday morning. The children were sitting at the kitchen table, finishing the last of their toast and jam, when they heard the key turn in the front door.

Mrs Harrison rushed to meet her husband immediately. 'Eric,' she said, 'are you all right? You look exhausted.'

'I'm all right,' replied Mr Harrison, but his voice betrayed the shock he had experienced. 'It's been a difficult night but I'm all right.'

He took off his coat and his boots, which were caked with dust and dirt, and he gave his wife a hug.

'We've been so worried about you,' she said. 'We've not been able to sleep, any of us. Alice has been in bed with me all night. Come in to the kitchen and tell us all about it.'

Mr Harrison pulled up a chair and joined the children at the kitchen table, while his wife poured him out a hot cup of tea.

'I still can't believe it,' he said, quietly. 'Three houses in Cotton Street completely destroyed and at least four others badly damaged. They'll probably have to come down. There were two direct hits. One of them hit Harry Wright's house - completely flattened it - I've never seen anything like it. Luckily, Harry had got the family out in time, but we had to dig them out of the Anderson shelter. The other got old Mr Hogg's place and it took out the house next door as well.'

At this point, Mr Harrison stopped and he lowered his head into his hands.

'Drink your tea,' urged his wife, and she put an arm around his shoulder.

Mr Harrison picked up the cup and sipped the hot, comforting liquid. John and Sparky glanced at each other, nervously, neither one wanting to ask the question that was haunting them. Still Mr Harrison paused and the tension became so great that John said, hesitantly:

'Can you tell us about . . . I mean, what happened to . . . is there any news of . . . '

'Are Janice and Mr Hogg safe?' said Sparky, decisively.

'Oh, yes, I'm sorry, I should have told you. They're both quite safe and unharmed. They're very shocked of course and they've been taken to Thornley hospital as a precaution. It seems that the old man heeded our warning and got down to the Anderson shelter. Thank goodness we went round to

119

talk to them the other day. They'll both be fine, although Mr Hogg's very upset about the dog.'

'The dog?' said John, slowly. 'What's happened to Betsy?'

'Went back into the house, apparently,' said Mr Harrison. 'When the first bombs dropped. They hadn't got time to go back for her. I suppose we should be thankful that the only serious casualty was a dog.'

John didn't hear the last sentence. He felt a lump in his throat and the tears welled up in his eyes. He stood up and rushed out of the kitchen, knocking his chair over in his haste to get up to his bedroom.

John didn't often cry. He usually mocked his sister Alice for bursting into tears at the slightest excuse, usually if she didn't get her own way. However, this Sunday morning he lay on his bed and sobbed to himself, quietly. After the chaos of the previous evening, everywhere seemed strangely still. In the distance, a church bell chimed, slowly and monotonously, as if it knew that this particular Sunday was not a call for celebration. John didn't want to be disturbed; he wanted to be alone with his thoughts. It was, therefore, with some irritation that on hearing a noise, he looked up from his bed to see Sparky's head poking around the bedroom door, his ridiculous glasses on the very end of his nose.

'Are you all right?' said Sparky, entering the room and adjusting his glasses. 'I thought I'd come and check that you're all right.'

'Thanks,' said John, sitting up and rubbing his eyes. 'I'll be fine. It's just that . . . '

'It doesn't seem fair,' completed Sparky. He sat on the bed and stared down at the floor. 'I know exactly what you mean, John. Mr Hogg's done nothing to harm anyone and yet he's lost his home and his best companion. It doesn't seem fair. And poor Janice. I know she can be a bit of a pain - but her parents sent her from Manchester to avoid the air raids and they go and bomb Thornley.'

'I hate this war,' said John, and he rubbed a few more tears from his eyes. 'I want things to be the way they were, before the war. What if there's an invasion? I overheard mum and dad talking the other morning and dad said the air raids were to soften us up before an invasion.'

'There won't be an invasion,' said Sparky, and he seemed to speak with confidence and certainty. 'I know there won't be an invasion.

That's why everyone in the country is joining together - to make sure that there won't be an invasion and to make sure that we win this war.'

'But everyone's not joining together, are they Sparky? Look what's happened to the ammunition trains in Liverpool and Coventry. Someone's passing information to German intelligence and it's costing lives as well as equipment.' John had stopped crying and his voice was angry and bitter. 'That's why Cotton Street was hit, Sparky. They were after the station and they hit Cotton Street instead. Janice and her grandad could have been killed.'

'I know that,' said Sparky, and he suddenly looked very uncomfortable. He stood up and walked across the room to the window. He stared out for a few moments and then he turned around to face John. 'There's something been bothering me,' he said. 'I was thinking about it last night when I couldn't sleep after the bombs fell.'

'Go on,' said John. 'I'm listening.'

Sparky moved forward and sat on the bed again. 'Well, we know that someone is passing information to the Germans - the times and the routes of the ammunition trains. Who would be in a position to do that,

John? It would have to be someone who could get hold of such confidential information - maybe someone working at the army base up on the moors - and even better if that person had a link to the railway station, don't you think?'

John's face had turned deathly pale. He looked at his friend and his mouth dropped open. He couldn't speak for a few moments but eventually he said: 'Sparky, you're not suggesting . . . '

'Think about it, John. A signalman who could stop the ammunition train so that it would be a sitting target. It makes sense, doesn't it?'

'But the army base . . . ' stammered John. 'Your own father . . . '

'Something's been nagging at me ever since I collected that package,' continued Sparky. 'Uncle Harry wouldn't tell me what it was but he stressed that it was very important and my father was very eager to collect it when he called to see us the other day. Suppose that package had something to do with . . . ' He left the sentence unfinished but John knew exactly what he was suggesting.

At that moment, there was a knock at the bedroom door and John's mum appeared carrying a tray of tea and cake. 'I've made you a nice hot cup of tea,' she said. 'This should cheer you up as well as warm you up.' She put the tray on the floor in front of them and picked up a plate on which were four thick slices of dark fruit cake. 'And this cake, Simon, is very special. Your father gave it to me on his way out the other morning. It's come all the way from your Auntie Edith down south. Remember, you collected it from the railway station the other evening, Simon? It was supposed to be a treat for them at the army base but your father thought we could make better use of it. Kind of him, wasn't it?'

Sparky and John took one look at the cake and they burst out laughing - and poor Mrs Harrison had not got a clue what they were laughing about!

There was a knock at the door soon after lunch. John had not eaten a great deal but for some reason, Sparky was starving and he had devoured John's sandwiches as well as his own. The two boys were just clearing the dishes away when Mrs Harrison entered the kitchen, followed by a large policeman. Sparky recognised him. It was the same policeman they had spoken to outside Mr

Hogg's house just after he had discovered that he had been robbed.

'This is constable Perkins,' explained Mrs Harrison. 'He wants to talk to you about the sack you discovered down by the lodge.'

The policeman looked like a Perkins. He had a pink face and big blue eyes.

'Actually, it's more than just talk,' beamed P.C. Perkins. 'I want you to accompany me down to the lodge and show me exactly where the sack is hidden - if that's all right with you, Mrs Harrison?'

'Er - yes, I suppose so,' said John's mum, looking flustered. 'It's just that Simon's father warned him not to go wandering off again. I promised I'd keep a firm watch over them both.'

Sparky frowned and glanced at John.

'Don't worry,' said P.C. Perkins, 'I can assure you they'll be quite all right with me. I'll have them back safe and sound within the hour.'

The day was still cold. It was not quite as clear as it had been of late. A bank of ash grey cloud was drifting in from the west. It had already covered the sun, so that the early afternoon was dull and miserable.

They passed the end of Cotton Street as they made their way down towards the lodge.

125

The whole street had been cordoned off. Sparky and John stopped and stared in horror at the smouldering pile of rubble that had once been people's homes. Several fire engines and an ambulance were on site and the boys could see the firemen sifting through the debris as neighbours stared in disbelief.

'Your friend's grandad was lucky last night,' said P.C. Perkins. 'He could have been buried under that lot.'

'Lucky?' repeated Sparky, shortly. 'His house has been completely destroyed. I wouldn't call that lucky, would you?'

'Yes, well - er, let's get on, should we?' said P.C. Perkins, awkwardly. 'Before the afternoon gets any darker.'

Another few minutes and they were on the rough track heading towards the footbridge. The afternoon was growing duller by the minute and P.C. Perkins set off along the track at a cracking pace, anxious to retrieve the sack as soon as possible and get it back to the station. John and Sparky trotted behind him, doing their best to keep up. Before long, the footbridge came into sight and P.C. Perkins stopped, suddenly, causing the boys to bump into the back of him. He stepped sideways towards the bushes and raised a warning hand.

'What's the matter?' said John. 'Can you see . . . '

'Someone on the bridge?' completed Sparky, and he nodded his head up and down. He had spotted the figure, too, leaning over the side of the stone bridge, peering down towards the stream.

'What's he doing?' asked John, straining his eyes to see more clearly.

'I'm not sure,' said P.C. Perkins. 'Let's get

closer. Keep into the bushes so that we don't disturb him.'

They moved forward, slowly and carefully, keeping to the edge of the bushes, getting even closer to the stone bridge. Sparky peered towards the figure and then nudged P.C. Perkins and whispered, 'I know him! It's Mr Stoppard, Bus Stop's dad.'

They edged closer still and then P.C. Perkins signalled for them to stop.

'There's someone under the bridge,' whispered Sparky, 'and I've a good idea who it is!'

They were close enough to hear Mr Stoppard speak.

'Will you get a move on, you stupid boy! I want to get that sack home before it gets dark.'

The next moment, he reached down and hauled the postman's sack up onto the top of the wall. 'About time!' he said, irritably, as Bus Stop appeared from the embankment and joined him on the bridge.

Bus Stop sat down on the wall and said, 'What happens now, dad? Do I get something out of this?'

'Of course you do, son. I've got someone collecting the stuff at 6 o'clock this evening. I'm sure I can sort out a nice surprise for you.'

'I think I can sort out a nice surprise for Mr Stoppard!' whispered P.C. Perkins. 'It's time to move in!'

'Can I have a bit of fun first,' said Sparky, and before the policeman could stop him, Sparky had stepped from the cover of the bushes and was striding out in full view towards the footbridge. 'Bus Stop!' shouted Sparky, and he waved his hand in the air as a greeting. 'Fancy seeing you here! Are you out for a walk with your father?'

Mr Stoppard stood bolt upright and tried to conceal the sack behind him. Bus Stop just sat on the wall with his mouth wide open. He looked like a village idiot.

'We're just going about our business,' stammered Mr Stoppard, 'before it gets too dark.'

'Going about your business?' repeated Sparky. 'Oh, I see! You're delivering letters, are you? Do you have a lot of letters to deliver to the deserted farmhouse?'

Sparky was on the bridge by now and he was staring around Mr Stoppard's legs at the postman's sack.

'Why don't you shove off?' said Bus Stop, finding his voice.

'No, why don't you shove off!' retorted Sparky, and he stepped forward and pushed the startled boy backwards over the bridge.

There was a yell and a thump as Bus Stop landed in the ice cold stream. Mr Stoppard couldn't believe his eyes. He leapt forward and grabbed hold of Sparky by the front of his jacket but a sharp voice stopped him in his tracks. P.C. Perkins was standing no more than a couple of yards away with his arms folded. Mr Stoppard let go of his hold and slumped to his knees with a dejected look on his face.

John rushed past P.C. Perkins and joined Sparky on the bridge. The two boys peered over the wall towards the stream, where Bus Stop was still sitting, shivering with cold, his thumb in his mouth and his other hand tugging at his big ear.

It was only when the boys had stopped laughing that Sparky peered over the gloomy fields towards Thornley Railway Station and noticed the bright light that was shining from Uncle Harry's signal box. Sparky didn't say a word but he felt a shiver run down his spine. It was a dull afternoon, they were bound to be able to see the signal box if Uncle Harry had the light switched on, yet something didn't feel right.

'Come on, you two,' said P.C. Perkins, he had hold of Mr Stoppard's arm and he was leading him from the bridge. 'I promised I'd have you back home within the hour. We'll have to get a move on.'

Sparky shook his head. 'We're on our way,' he said. 'We're right behind you.'

Chapter 11

The Ammunition Train

The more Sparky thought about it, the more it bothered him. He hadn't said anything to John but he couldn't understand why the signal box seemed to be so brightly lit. When they had visited Uncle Harry, just a few days ago, to collect the package, there had been one dull bulb hanging from the ceiling. All right, the bulb might have blown but why replace it with one so much more powerful? He wondered, for a moment, if there could be any connection to the ammunition train - but that wasn't due through the station until tomorrow - Monday, the day that was circled on the railway timetable. He dismissed the thought from his mind but the light still bothered him.

They had gone with P.C. Perkins and his two prisoners back to the police station. Bus Stop looked totally dejected. He was soaking wet and shivering. He kept pulling at his ear and glaring at Sparky as though he would ring his neck if he were given half a chance. Mr Stoppard denied everything. He claimed that he had just gone out for a walk with his son and that they had spotted the sack at the bottom of the embankment. He assured P.C. Perkins that they were about to bring it in to the police station as they were responsible citizens. He was stunned when P.C. Perkins told him that Bus Stop and his friends had been seen with the sack in that very spot the previous day.

Mr Harrison returned home early. It was just five-thirty. John and Sparky were playing a game of Ludo with Alice when he entered the living room and greeted them.

'I wasn't expecting you home until seven o'clock,' said John's mum. 'I haven't got your dinner ready.'

'There's been a change of plan,' explained Mr Harrison. 'It's all been top secret and we've only just got to know. The ammunition train is coming through Thornley Station at nine o'clock tonight. They've brought the date forward by one day. All the wardens have got to report for duty in case there's an air raid.'

Sparky's face turned deathly white. He opened his mouth to say something but no words came out. John could see him struggling for breath and he said, 'Sparky, are you all right? You look awful!'

Sparky sprung to his feet and rushed out of the room, scattering the Ludo board in his haste to get away.

'Look what he's done!' cried Alice. 'He's spoilt our game and I was winning!'

'Perhaps he's not feeling too well,' said Mrs Harrison, looking concerned. 'Go and check he's all right, John.'

John left the room and followed Sparky upstairs to the bedroom. He opened the door cautiously, to see his friend sitting on the bed, still deathly white and shaking.

'Whatever's the matter, Sparky? You look as if you've seen a ghost!'

'There's something wrong, John.' Sparky fiddled with his glasses. His voice was trembling. 'The ammunition train's coming through Thornley tonight.'

'Well, what's wrong with that?' asked John. 'You should be pleased, especially if you still think those two strangers we saw on the bridge were spies. They'll be expecting the train to come through tomorrow. They circled tomorrow's date on the timetable. We passed it on to your father, remember?'

'When we were leaving the footbridge earlier this afternoon,' began Sparky, 'I noticed a bright light coming from the signal box next to the station. Don't you think that's strange, John?'

His friend looked puzzled. 'I don't understand, Sparky. What are you trying to say?'

'Surely the railway station would be the last place anyone would want brightly lit, especially with an ammunition train due to pass through. Unless, that is, someone wanted to draw attention to the station, mark it out as a target so that it could be clearly seen, even from the sky.'

John looked horrified. He walked further into the room and sat on the bed next to Sparky. 'What are you suggesting?' he said. 'Your Uncle Harry . . . and your own father? Surely you still don't think . . . '

'Yes . . . No . . . I, I just don't know,' interrupted Sparky. 'But I'm sure there's something wrong and we've got to do something about it, John. We'd never forgive ourselves if the train was bombed and we hadn't warned anyone.'

'O.K.,' said John, standing up and walking towards the bedroom door, 'we'll tell my father. He'll know what to do. After all, he is an A.R.P. warden.'

John headed for the bedroom door and Sparky followed him. As they descended the stairs, John's mum was standing at the bottom, looking worried.

'Are you all right, Simon?' she said. 'Rushing out like that - it's not like you. You're not ill, are you?'

'I'm fine,' lied Sparky. 'We'd just like to have a word with Mr Harrison, if that's all right, before he goes back on duty.'

'I'm sorry, you've just missed him. Didn't you hear him call up to say goodbye? He only set off a couple of minutes ago. I suggest you two have an early night, just in case the bombers return and we have to go down to the shelter again. You look tired, both of you - and it's school in the morning, you know.'

Mrs Harrison disappeared into the living room to see to Alice and both John and Sparky sat down on the stairs without saying a word. John stared at the front door, as if he was willing his father to walk back through into the hallway - but no one appeared.

'There's only one thing for it,' said Sparky, after a couple of minutes. 'I'll have to go down to the railway station and check it out for myself.'

John nearly choked. He spluttered and coughed and then said, 'Are you absolutely mad? What if the bombers come over? Besides, my mum will never agree to you going out at this time of evening, especially as she promised your father she'd keep a close watch over you. You've no chance.'

'I'm not thinking of asking her,' said

Sparky. 'And I'm not thinking of going yet.' His plan was coming together. 'We'll wait until Alice has gone to bed and we'll tell your mother we're going to have that early night she suggested. Once she thinks we're settled, we'll be able to sneak past the living room and out of the back door. We can check out the station and be back before she even realises we've gone.'

'Wait a minute,' said John, putting a hand on Sparky's shoulder, 'what do you mean *we*?'

'I know you'll come with me,' said Sparky, confidently. 'You wouldn't let me go on my own, would you John?'

His friend didn't answer. Instead he said, 'And what do you mean *check out the station*? What exactly do you plan to do?'

'It's simple,' explained Sparky. 'Lights aren't allowed during blackout. If we go to the station and find that it's in darkness then we'll know that everything is all right. In that case, I'll admit that I was fussing about nothing and we'll turn round and come straight home.'

'But what if the lights are on?' said John. 'What do we do then?'

'We'll go straight to Thornley Police Station and talk to P.C. Perkins,' said Sparky, 'or to that nice sergeant we met yesterday.'

John thought for a few moments and then he said, 'I hope the lights are off, Sparky. I really hope the lights are off.'

Everything went according to plan. The boys had a hot drink and then they went up to their room. Alice was already tucked up in bed, fast asleep. It was approaching eight o'clock. The ammunition train was due to pass through Thornley Station in less than one hour. They would need to move quickly. Sparky walked across to the window and looked up to the night sky. The weather was definitely changing. Broken clouds scurried across a cold moon.

Turning back to John, he said, 'It's time to go. Are you still with me?'

'As quiet as possible,' said John, by way of answer. 'The third stair from the bottom creaks so make sure you miss it out.'

They slipped on their jackets, which they had brought upstairs to save time. Sparky could still feel the weight of Mr Hogg's watch and chain in his pocket and he thought that it might be useful to keep an eye on the time. The two boys opened the bedroom door and stood at the top of the stairs, listening. Mrs Harrison was in the living room and she had the radio switched on. Good! That would make it easier to sneak past her. They descended the stairs slowly and cautiously, remembering to avoid the third step from the bottom. John put his ear to the living room door and nodded in satisfaction as he heard Vera Lynne singing one of his mother's favourite songs. A few more steps and they were in the kitchen and they could breathe more easily. John didn't switch the light on. He fumbled towards the back door, turned the key in the lock and the boys stepped out into the night.

It was strange walking along the familiar streets in the dark. There were no street lights and the houses were in almost total darkness, the occasional thin chink of light finding its way through a gap in the blackout curtains. They passed the school and they passed the end of Cotton Street, which was still cordoned off so that no one could reach the bomb site. As they approached the railway station Sparky's heart began to beat faster. The ammunition train was due through before nine o'clock. He pulled Mr Hogg's watch and chain from his pocket and saw that it was twenty minutes past eight. That wouldn't give them long to get to the police station if there was a problem.

And then they stopped, suddenly, as if frozen by fear. The air raid siren cut into the night, groaning at first and then rising to a screaming crescendo. It seemed louder than ever now that they were out in the open, away from the houses.

John grabbed his friend's arm, a look of sheer panic on his face. 'What shall we do, Sparky? The bombers are on the way!'

'We're nearly there,' yelled Sparky. 'A quick check at the station and we'll get back. Come on!'

He set off at a run and John chased after him, wishing he was anywhere but out on the open streets. The wailing siren seemed to follow them as they dashed towards the station. And then they were there, at the entrance, and to Sparky's relief it was in darkness.

Sparky put his hands to his eyes and peered through the double doors towards the ticket booth and the main office. 'I can't see a thing,' he said. 'Everywhere's dark.'

'That's good,' replied John. 'Let's get home, Sparky. Mum will be going frantic. I'm in enough trouble as it is.'

'Wait,' said Sparky. 'Something's not right. The doors are locked.'

'It's probably for security,' said John

140

'There's an ammunition train coming through, don't forget.'

Sparky moved away from the doors and stood by the brick wall that ran the length of the platform. 'Give me a lift up,' he yelled to John, 'so that I can see over the wall.'

'Sparky, the bombers are coming! We need to get back home!' But seeing the determined look on his friend's face he said, 'Oh, what's the use!'

John moved forward and cupped his hands together to give Sparky a lift. It was easy. Sparky put one foot into John's cradled hands and pulled himself up so that he could just see over the top of the wall.

In the distance the unmistakable drone that signalled the arrival of the bombers could just be heard.

Sparky peered onto the platform and then down the line towards the signal box. 'It's lit!' he gasped. 'There's a bright light in the signal box, John - and the bombers are coming!'

At the same time, a new sound could be heard and, to Sparky, it was every bit as frightening as the bombers' drone. It was a steady, rhythmic sound that grew gradually louder and then slowed as it approached the station. Sparky stared along the line in horror as the ammunition train approached like a great metal monster. He watched open mouthed as the steam from the engine rose in white clouds into the night sky and his blood ran cold as the train ground to a halt on the railway bridge beyond the signal box.

'I can't hold you!' yelled John from below. 'You're too heavy, Sparky!'

Sparky let go his grip on the wall and stepped out of John's cradled hands. 'The ammunition train's on the bridge,' he panted. 'The signal must have brought it to a halt.'

'We've got to get help,' gasped John. 'The bombers are coming. If they hit the train . . .'

'We've no time to get help,' yelled Sparky. 'The German pilots will be able to see the light from the signal box. They're going to bomb the train, John! They're going to bomb the train!'

There was a sudden blast from the whistle of the ammunition train as the driver realised he was stuck on the bridge and, as the blast faded, the drone of the bombers approaching grew ever louder.

Sparky made up his mind. 'Give me a lift onto the top of the wall,' he snapped. 'As soon as I'm over, run as fast as you can to the police station and get help.'

John looked horrified. 'Sparky, you can't! You could get yourself killed!'

142

'Come on!' yelled Sparky. 'Give me a lift!'

It was no use arguing. John clasped his hands together again, Sparky stepped into the cradle and he was up onto the wall in seconds, forgetting all about his fear of heights.

'Now go!' ordered Sparky, and he watched as John ran away into the darkness for all he was worth.

Sparky jumped down onto the platform and glanced around quickly. The entrance area was in total darkness but the signal box shone like a beacon into the night sky. The bombers would arrive over Thornley any minute. Where was Bloch, the station master? Why hadn't he prevented Uncle Harry from stopping the ammunition train on the bridge? It was a sitting target!

The first bombs dropped somewhere across Thornley, a series of explosions rocking the night and stirring Sparky into action. He raced along the platform towards the signal box, keeping close in to the wall. He leapt down onto the gravel track, as the train whistle screamed again into the night sky. And then, as he neared the wooden steps, he could see a figure in the signal box, silhouetted in the bright light. The figure was standing very still, staring up the track towards the bridge, hands clasped around the signal control lever.

Another cluster of bombs dropped, nearer, louder, ripping into the battered town.

Sparky crept up the steps and peered through the window in the top half of the wooden door - and gasped as he recognised the figure as Bloch, the stationmaster. A body was sprawled out on the floor of the signal box and, although it was face down, Sparky knew that it was Uncle Harry.

Sparky acted instinctively. He flung open the wooden door and charged towards Bloch with a blood curdling yell. But the stationmaster was too strong for him; Bloch swung his arm at the last second and caught Sparky with a vicious blow that sent him sprawling across the signal box. Sparky was down, crumpled on the floor in front of the open door.

'You!' screamed Bloch. 'What are you doing here?'

Sparky shook himself as the big man advanced, a look of hate on his distorted face. Sparky reached into his pocket and withdrew the watch and chain he still carried with him. Bloch charged and Sparky swung his weapon. The solid silver watch thumped against the side of the stationmaster's head, stopping him in his tracks. His mouth opened, his eyes widened and he staggered forward. Sparky rolled out of his way as he stumbled through the open doorway, tottered for a moment and then tumbled down the wooden steps, crashing in a heap at the bottom.

Sparky's heart was racing. He knew the bombers were almost overhead. He leapt towards the signal controls and grabbed the lever. He knew what to do; his Uncle Harry had showed him. He had to move the train through the station. But the lever was jammed; he tugged and strained but he couldn't budge it. Sparky fell to the floor and shook Uncle Harry. It was no good; he was out cold.

And then a huge explosion shook the signal box, sending Sparky reeling across the wooden floor. He staggered to his feet, realising that the light from the signal box was guiding the bombers. He snapped off the switch and leapt down the wooden steps, over the motionless body of the stationmaster.

He was on the railway track within seconds, running for all he was worth towards the ammunition train, yelling to attract the driver's attention, his heart pounding, his lungs bursting.

Sparky was nearly there. He slowed to a stagger and stood before the great, black engine. And then a figure emerged from the shadows and limped towards the exhausted boy, as the bombers roared overhead. Sparky recognised the German pilot immediately, his clothes torn, his face still bloodied from the crash on the moors.

Sparky couldn't move. He stood, transfixed, as the figure advanced relentlessly towards him.

The last thing Sparky remembered was the chilling whistling sound and the force of the blast as the bomb hit its target. It was almost as if it happened in slow motion. There was a blinding flash and he felt himself reeling backwards and then there was nothing. Nothing except total blackness.

Chapter 12

Heaven or Hell?

John had burst through the doors of Thornley Police Station and almost collapsed on the counter.

'You've got to help me!' he gasped. 'The bombers are coming . . . and the ammunition train is on the bridge . . . they'll see the light . . . and Sparky's climbed over the wall, and . . . '

'Hold on a minute, young man! Just hold your horses!' It was the sergeant, the same sergeant that had been in on the interview the previous day. 'What on earth are you doing out on the streets at this time? Didn't you hear the sirens?'

'I'm trying to tell you!' shouted John. He was shaking with frustration. He took a deep breath and began again. 'We saw a bright light in the railway signal box this afternoon, when we were with P.C. Perkins down by Thornley Lodge. Sparky thought there was something wrong then and, when he heard that the ammunition train was coming through the station a day early, he put two and two together. Don't you see! It's a signal for the bombers! The light will guide them!

They're going to destroy the train!'

The blood drained from the sergeant's face. Outside, the explosions had begun and the police station shook as each blast got nearer.

'Wait here!' snapped the sergeant, and he disappeared into a back room. He was out again within seconds, two burly policemen following him through the door. 'Come on!' said the sergeant. 'You can show me where your friend went over the wall.'

The railway station was just three streets away and they raced through the night, the frightening sound of the approaching bombers getting closer with every second. Dark clouds scuddered across the moon. It was no longer a bombers' moon but the planes wouldn't need that - they had the light from the signal box to guide them.

They were there within minutes and John showed the officers where Sparky had disappeared over the wall.

'We'll use the front entrance,' yelled the sergeant. He glanced up. The bombers were in the sky. They were almost directly over the station.

'It's locked!' yelled John. 'The front entrance is locked! That's why Sparky went over the wall!'

'Keep behind us!' snapped the policeman.

John watched as the sergeant tried the door and then nodded at the two officers. Together, they charged forward and burst it open with ease, the two sections flying inwards in a mass of splinters.

'Come on!' yelled the sergeant, and they raced through the entrance area past the ticket booth and the main office.

A cluster of bombs fell nearby, rocking the station and stopping them in their tracks for a moment. John was the first to move, rushing forward past the officers onto the deserted platform. 'Look!' he shouted, and he pointed towards the signal box that shone like a beacon in the darkness. Beyond the box, in the distance, they could see the ammunition train waiting on the bridge, as above their heads another wave of bombers closed in on their target.

Another massive explosion threw them to the ground. It was close; very close. It must have hit one of the streets right next to the station. John got up and shook himself and when he looked back towards the signal box, the light had gone out. Had that been caused by the bomb blast or had somebody switched it off? Now they couldn't see a thing. The clouds had covered the moon and now the signal box, the track and the ammunition train were in complete darkness.

'You wait here,' ordered the sergeant, as they reached the end of the platform. 'It will be safer. We'll go and check out the signal box.'

The officers descended the wooden steps from the platform onto the rough track that led them to the signal box. There was no way John was staying behind. He jumped down after them and followed a few paces behind, the bombers droning ominously loud overhead.

As they neared the signal box, the sergeant quickened his pace. He had spotted the slumped figure lying at the bottom of the steps. He knelt down and pulled the body over.

'It's Bloch!' he gasped. 'It's the stationmaster! Somebody's knocked him out!'

At that moment, the clouds cleared from the moon and a pale light lit up the eerie scene. John glanced along the track towards the train, fearing for its safety, and his blood froze in horror. A small figure was on the track itself, hurrying towards the waiting train. The officers saw it too, ghostly in the pale moonlight. The figure stopped as a darker, more threatening shape emerged from the embankment and stumbled onto the track.

A sudden, chilling, whistling sound shook John with terror. He screamed into the night.

'Sparky! No-o-o! Sparky!' His scream was lost in the all-enveloping explosion.

Sparky wasn't sure whether or not he was in heaven. He wasn't moving and yet there were strange bright lights, flashing lights that seemed to zoom towards the front of his head before fading away again. There was a strange noise, too; a constant buzzing, as if there was a giant bee stuck in his ear. He wanted to stick a finger in his ear and wiggle it about but he found that he couldn't lift his arm. No, he couldn't be in heaven. It was a really unpleasant noise that wouldn't go away and there was a stabbing pain from his arm when he tried to lift it. Perhaps he was in the other place. Perhaps he was in hell!

A voice invaded his thoughts, a familiar high pitched voice that seemed to confirm that Sparky was indeed in hell.

'Simon! Can you hear me, Simon? Everything's going to be fine. We're right here by your side!'

Janice Hogg leaned forward and put a hand on Sparky's arm.

'What are you doing here?' said Sparky. His voice was weak and his mouth felt dry. 'And who else is with you? Come to think of it, what am I doing here? Where am I?'

'You're in Thornley Hospital, Simon. Don't you remember the explosion? John's here with your father. They've just gone to get a cup of tea. You've been unconscious since they brought you in last night. We're in the same hospital together, Simon. That's nice, isn't it?'

'Wonderful!' said Sparky, unconvincingly.

'My grandad's here as well,' continued Janice. 'He's all right, just very shaken. He's lost the house, though. He's going to come and live with us in Manchester.'

Sparky was just thinking that he preferred the bright lights and the buzzing sound to Janice's voice when John and his father returned.

'Sparky! You're back with us,' said John. 'We were a bit worried about you.'

'Hello, son,' said Sparky's dad. 'How are you feeling?'

'O.K., I think,' said Sparky. 'Why can't I see anything?'

'You've got bandages over your eyes,' explained Mr Parks. 'I'm afraid you've got a broken arm and a fair few bruises as well. The doctors say you'll make a full recovery but you've had a narrow escape.'

'I couldn't stop the train from blowing up,' said Sparky, remembering. 'What about all the people?'

'There was no one left on the train when it blew,' said Sparky's dad. 'The crew knew there was something wrong and they escaped over the far end of the bridge before the bomb hit. It was just as well - the bridge was completely destroyed. What was left of the train plunged down to the road. Amazingly, there was only one casualty and that was the German pilot. He didn't make it, I'm afraid.'

'And Uncle Harry?' said Sparky. 'He was on the signal box floor. What about Uncle Harry?'

'Your Uncle Harry's fine,' said Sparky's dad. 'He'll have a bit of a sore head for a while but they've let him go home this morning.'

'You frightened the life out of us,' chipped in John. 'And you should have heard what my mum and dad had to say about you!'

'I can imagine,' said Sparky, and he tried to laugh until he realised that it hurt. 'I don't suppose I'll be very welcome in your house when I get out of hospital, will I?'

'Well actually,' began Mr Parks, 'we won't be staying in Thornley, Simon. Now that we've got Bloch I'm being posted elsewhere. It looks as if we could be going back down south.'

'Down south?' repeated Janice, looking disappointed. 'That's a shame, isn't it, Simon? We won't be able to see each other.'

'That is a shame,' said Sparky, quietly - but Janice couldn't help but notice a thin smile creep across his face.

The End